It is 1945. The camp on Bloc

areas on the Malayan Penir
surrender has not yet penetra
earth for several hundred r
nations, trapped during the J
under conditions of cruelty,

The prisoners – held in
despair, almost praying for
appalling ordeal. Only Colon
camp, and Van Elst, a for[illegible] planter, know that the war is over. Lambert knows, too, that every prisoner will be slaughtered immediately Colonel Yamamitsu, the gross, brutal commandant of the camp, learns of the Japanese defeat ...

J. M. White and
Val Guest

The Camp on Blood Island

Based on a screenplay by
the Authors

A MAYFLOWER BOOK

GRANADA
London Toronto Sydney New York

Published by Granada Publishing Limited in 1972
Reprinted 1982

ISBN 0 583 12004 0

First published in Great Britain by
Panther Books Ltd 1958
Reprinted 1958 (eight times), 1959 (twice)
Panther new edition published 1959
Reprinted 1960, 1961, 1962 (twice), 1963, 1965, 1966, 1967, 1968, 1970, 1971

Granada Publishing Limited
Frogmore, St Albans, Herts AL2 2NF
and
36 Golden Square, London W1R 4AH
866 United Nations Plaza, New York, NY 10017, USA
117 York Street, Sydney, NSW 2000, Australia
100 Skyway Avenue, Rexdale, Ontario, M9W 3A6, Canada
61 Beach Road, Auckland, New Zealand

Printed and bound in Great Britain by
Cox & Wyman Ltd, Reading
Set in Monotype Plantin

The Camp on Blood Island

Introduction

THESE words were carved on a crude wooden door on a December morning in 1942.

> "Sometimes they shut you up in jail—
> Dark, and a filthy cell;
> I hope the fellows that built them jails,
> Find 'em down in Hell."

The door was the only entrance to a crude wooden hut. Around it were scores of similar huts. Around them was a high wire fence. Inside that fence were hundreds of people; all different, but made uniform by a bond of suffering.

They were prisoners of the Japanese.

They had been captured during the long and bitter fight for the Malay Peninsula. They were a mixture of soldiers and civilians; men, women and children. There were scores of such camps wherever the yellow men had conquered. These camps were the most infamous in the world. And those words, carved by a soldier hours before he was beheaded, are an immortal epitaph to the depravity of the Japanese. Nowhere was that depravity more marked than in the Malay Peninsula.

We have examined the sworn testimony of some of those who survived. It is a sickening catalogue of unbelievable bestiality. We found much evidence of murder, rape and torture.

This book is an attempt to present—fully and authentically—a picture of what the British Government called, "the most vile savagery the world has ever known." This is not a pretty story; but violence in any degree is never picturesque. Though this is the personal story of only a few who fell under the yellow lash it is typical of the fate of most. Yet this book is important, if only for the reason that it prompts the question: "What happened to those who committed these atrocities?"

Bluntly, the answer is NOTHING.

Worse, we have evidence that many of those who escaped the

few War Crimes Trials held in Tokyo in 1946 are today in a position that gives them their previous powers over foreign nationals. That power was given to them by the man who became known as the Liberator of the East—General Douglas MacArthur. It was a grim-faced MacArthur who arrived in Tokyo in 1945 and saw the evidence of the concentration camps and said that "never again must this happen".

And yet in October 1950—five short years after the horrors documented in this book—MacArthur announced that all British and other nationals would be "subjected to the jurisdiction of Japanese courts in criminal cases."

MacArthur justified this by saying he believed in "the legal, judicial and police institutions" of Japan. He vouched for their ability to "execute responsibility impartially, fairly and with justice."

That, we feel, was the most monstrous decision taken by any supreme commander in an occupied country.

For power was invested in the hands of those who had so wantonly abused it during the last war. Many of the concentration camp guards had joined the post-war National Police Reserve. On March 20, 1952 *The Times* reported its strength as 75,000, adding that it included former Imperial Army officers up to the rank of colonel.

But the brunt of this force—it is really a small but well equipped Army—had belonged to the once all-powerful Kempei Organisation. The Kempei were directly responsible for all the atrocities committed against Allied prisoners. It was this organisation that encouraged torture of all sorts. A typical example was a Kempei report which urged camp guards to commit vile assaults on women prisoners.

The powers of the Kempei were far, far greater than those of the Gestapo. Several members of the organisation were attached to all concentration camps. Their task was to see that there was no letting-up in the atrocities. They tried to disguise this task by calling it counter-espionage work, but nobody—least of all the captives—was hoodwinked. After the war these men went underground—only to reappear in the National Police Force. It was the chance they had been waiting for; the chance to practise still more ill-treatment. The zealous MacArthur must be held responsible for giving them their chance.

And in Britain—a country which had suffered greatly at the hands of the Japanese—only one voice protested. A Sunday newspaper said that injustice could result from "this extraordinary state of affairs!"

That must be the understatement of many a Sunday for this newspaper. It will bring a sallow smile to the lips of all those who survived the horror camps of the East.

GORDON THOMAS.
ARTHUR KENT.

Chapter One

1

It was a good day to die on Blood Island. The sun had a too-brassy glare and the air was like steam coming out of a green mist. The island lay about fifty miles south of the foot of the Malay Peninsula. It was a lop-sided tract of land that in many ways resembled the end of the world: the sky and earth melted into a landscape that was pre-historic. From whatever way it was approached the island had a barbaric look about it.

It was barbaric. For it was the setting for one of the most infamous prisoner-of-war experiments that the Japanese ever tried.

Late in 1942 the little yellow men had escorted hundreds of men, women and children on to the island. Then they had beaten them and raped them while the prisoners, of all nations, had built their own camps. The men built one at the southern end of the island. The women theirs at the northern end. During the building the nameless island had been named Blood Island. But to the Japanese it was the Island of Paradise. As well as the lush tropical foliage there was human entertainment. The guards never tired of savaging the inmates of the male compound, while those held in the female camp provided them with unlimited practice in fornicating. No Japanese could ask for more. Except, of course, a special execution, on a day that was too hot and too humid....

2

The spade was heavy, too heavy. It only bit spasmodically into the hard, sun-dried dirt. He lifted the spade and the effort brought the sweat seeping out on to his thin, emaciated body. He told himself that it was a dream. That any moment now he would wake up and find himself upright in his bed, wondering why he had dreamt such a dream. Wondering why he had convinced himself that it was a good day to die.

"Of course it is," he croaked. The words were bright shattering reality. The spade was real, so was the sweat and tears. So was the hole beneath him—his own grave. And as he looked up from his digging he saw the three yellow men, grinning like idiots, in their shapeless and almost comic uniforms. They were banked behind a machine gun. He noticed that its barrel was constantly trained on his stomach. It made him feel sick; the vomit had actually reached his throat before he checked the emotion.

Lieutenant John Davies, formerly of His Majesty's Militia at Singapore and bank clerk at one of the branches in the Far East of a big British Bank, detested emotion in any shape or form. He told himself that the tears running down his face were really beads of perspiration. He told himself once more that it was a good day to die—and be freed from the torture, the heat, the privations, the fetid swamps, the monsoon. Against that death was not unwelcome. But he was troubled by the manner of his dying and the thought of what came after. When he had thought of death—which had been often in the three years he had been immured on Blood Island—he had hoped that it would be an orderly one, and if there was a chance, he would have liked a say in the way he was to die.

But this . . . and the tears flowed a little faster.

"Bloody sweat," he shouted, "Dirty, bloody sweat."

"No talk! Dig, faster, faster," ordered one of the machine-gunners in a bastardisation of the English language that the Japanese felt was the correct way to address a foreigner.

"Balls!"

"No balls. Dig, faster, faster," came the solemn reply.

What a way to die. Davies thought, bitterly. If only he had strength from some hidden reservoir, he could grab one of the guards and take one with him to his death. But they were too far away. The ground was bumpy, shaped by the graves of those who lay beneath the soil. All had died at special executions.

Davies rested for a moment, bent almost double over the roughly shaped handle of his spade. For the past three years he had watched scores of other men bent in the same position as they had almost completed their graves. There had been Adams; he had died with a wild Highland curse on his lips. Jenkins had been cut down with an air of dignity about him. He had been known as the "Parson". Watkins had screamed before the gunners silenced him. He was only a youth. There were others too: Partingdon, a wispy-haired soldier from

Belfast; Young, a mountain of a man, who had yelled "Christ!" and had died during his futile charge at the gunners. Marshall had died urinating. He had told the guards that he insisted on watering his grave. Davies remembered them all. And soon he knew he could go the way they had gone. His only choice in the matter was how he would go.

But he knew that whatever way he chose, there would always be Captain Sakamura to take into account.

"Dig, faster, faster," shouted a gunner. "No need delay. You die all same."

"Sakamura getting impatient?"

"So so. Hurry, hurry."

Yes, thought Davies, Sakamura would be getting impatient. He loved special executions. He staged them with commendable skill. He had an audience—all the prisoners were given time off to attend the show. He had an impresario's touch for the right moment to order the show to reach its climax.

Davies remembered that somebody had once summed up Sakamura's philosophy thus, "Some men like Shakespeare. Others leggy revues. Some like to get drunk in Chinese brothels. Some like reading books. Captain Sakamura likes staging special executions."

As he looked up he saw that Sakamura had arrived to stage-manage and present his latest show. The Captain was strutting back and forth behind the machine-gunners, rubbing his hands and beaming at the prisoners lined up behind the barbed wire fence.

"See," shouted Sakamura, "It is easy to get out of this camp. Just volunteer for a special execution. Very quick, also very clean." He roared with laughter.

The noise evaporated what little strength, courage and hatred Davies had mustered in the past minutes. The three men behind the machine-gun he didn't know or care about. They were colourless, unidentifiable. But Sakamura was different. Davies had lived beneath his cruelty for three years and he knew that the Captain was invincible. He was the devil. A devil that in the past three years had become a god, to be feared, avoided, but never offended.

Three years. To Davies they seemed like three centuries. Surely more than three years had passed since he had slept in a decent bed, worn fine clothes, eaten well, felt the touch of a woman. It seemed much longer. Much, much longer. His previous life in Singapore and London seemed unreal, as if he was looking back on something so fantastic that he could only imagine it. Finally he decided that for him, Singapore and London had never been.

He had spent all his life on this farm where he was treated as little more than an animal. He had always been an animal. And now he was going the way of all beasts—through the slaughter yard. And yet animal though he might be, Davies still felt that he ought to die with more than an animal's dignity.

He let the knife-like edge of the spade fall through the dug earth. The weight of the spade, more than any pressure he applied to it, pushed it down. The grave was very shallow, he thought, and he had been a long time about it. A strange thought crossed his mind. It must be deeper. It could get very cold at night. The thought took a grip on him and became an obsession. He began to dig with a frenzy, slashing at the soil. He began to mutter to himself.

Sakamura saw the change and became bored. There was no more entertainment in a man who had gone mad. The Captain looked round. Everything was ready and in place. He saw the straggling line of prisoners behind the wire. He looked towards Colonel Yamamitsu's bungalow and saw that the fat interpreter was on the verandah, ready to fetch the camp commandant when Sakamura gave the signal.

The Captain lifted his hand and waggled his wrist. It was a curiously effeminate gesture. The interpreter went into the bungalow. As he went, Sakamura smiled to himself. The Colonel liked prawns. Most of the day Yamamitsu sat behind his large desk and ate prawns. Sakamura hoped that his Colonel would be disturbed in the middle of one of these dishes. He didn't like his Colonel. It was not so much a dislike as a hatred, deep and pathological. He hated the Colonel, not for anything the man had done to him, but because Sakamura thought he was a better man.

The prisoners stiffened when they saw the signal. The line, despite the ragged condition of the men, appeared to straighten slightly. There came an almost indistinguishable murmur. Some of the apathy left the men. But only pity—and not much of that—showed on their faces as they looked at Davies; abandoned, alone, working among the mounds of earth at the final preparations of his special execution.

3

Colonel Yamamitsu turned away from the long window of the house when the interpreter entered and bowed. The Colonel knew what the man had come for. He had been watching the preparations for the past half-hour. It had surprised Yamamitsu that his deputy could find so much pleasure in the sordid business. It also worried him. For he knew that Sakamura could be a danger to himself. And the Colonel didn't like the idea of being cornered by his homicidal deputy. The war was nearing its end, and the Allies were winning. Few Japanese officers would admit this to themselves, let alone discuss it. The Kempei Organisation executed anybody who even breathed a word about the possibility that the Rising Sun would founder. But Yamamitsu considered himself neither a fanatic nor fool. He knew the end was near. He knew too that there would be much to answer for. There had been many, many atrocities committed under his command, both at this camp and the women's camp. He knew that the Allies would seek retribution. The thought had started to give the Colonel sleepless nights. His prawns and saki had lost some of their pungent flavour. Sakamura's continued revelling in special executions did little to make him feel better.

At first he hadn't minded the Captain's periodic butchering. He had not actually approved the idea, for the more prisoners he had under his command, the more important his position seemed to be in far-off Tokyo. And he had played with the thought that if Sakamura slaughtered too many prisoners, the camp would be merged with another or placed under the command of an officer of lower rank, and he would be shifted to the war front.

But that had been in the early days when the Imperial Japanese Army had been swarming across the Asiatic continent towards India and pincering out towards Australia, the East Indies. And what happened to the defeated enemy was of no consequence. The Colonel knew how soft Europeans were. He knew that if he was captured he would be well treated, for the Europeans fought within the confines of rules and regulations. A fact that had always puzzled the Colonel. But there were risks to be faced. He knew that out in the surrounding jungle there was an ever-growing army of escaped prisoners and trained saboteurs. They had few arms, but they were in contact with the advancing Allies. He knew that if they got hold of him before the Allied soldiers did, he would have a quick, probably unpleasant, death.

It made him feel uncomfortable. And it brought back to his mind the problem that had nagged at him for the past few weeks. The problem of what to do with the prisoners. He had thought of giving Sakamura a blood-bath, allowing him to execute all the captives by whichever method he desired. The Captain had suggested the idea several times. He had sounded like a schoolboy, eager for a special treat. After the executions, all the evidence could be burnt. The idea had a definite appeal for the Colonel. Dead men tell no tales, he mused, was an old Western saying. But he felt he should consider the matter a little more, seeing if there were any unseen difficulties for his personal future.

The arrival of the interpreter interrupted his train of thought.

"Speak," he snapped. "Hurry!"

"Your Excellency. The execution is about to take place."

The Colonel nodded. He picked up his gloves and marched towards the door. He reached the verandah. Two sentries presented arms in a sloppy, desultory fashion. Yamamitsu looked at the shambling line of prisoners and lifted his head nervously towards the machine-gun nests on the pillars along the wire, then looked at Sakamura. The Captain beamed at his superior. And Yamamitsu gave the impression that he was paying special attention to everything going on. But his thoughts were far away from things unpleasant. He had had enough of worrying for one day. Executions, and the advancing Allies could wait. His mind was now on pleasure. On prawns. On saki. And on the white girl he had taken from the women's compound two years before—and who now lived in his bungalow.

The memory of that girl made him feel slightly hot and sticky. A sensual quiver thrilled through his body. It brought back memories of that morning two years before when he had marched into the women's stockade. All the women had been lined up. There had been about three hundred of them. Like a cattle buyer selecting from a herd, Yamamitsu had walked slowly up and down the line. The old he had discarded. The too young he had noted for future use. He knew what he wanted. A white girl, about eighteen, well built. With a big bust. That was important. Japanese women had small breasts. The Colonel wanted a change. It had taken him two hours to find the right kind of girl. In many ways it had been an enjoyable two hours. He had fingered and fondled several of the "possibles" before settling on his final choice.

It still made him smile when he remembered her reaction. She had spat in his face and swore at him. He had smiled. He liked a woman with spirit. But he also liked discipline. So he had watched while two guards had disciplined the girl. A whip had done the trick in remarkably quick time.

Then the girl had been carried back to his bungalow and to his bedroom. Again she had struggled. But this time the Colonel had dealt with her himself. The memory of how he had torn her dress off was still a pleasurable one. That was the only time she had struggled. Now, he reflected, she almost looked forward to his joining her in bed. Women, he mused, are funny. . . .

4

Captain Sakamura flipped back his cuff and looked at the time on his solid gold wrist-watch. It was a good watch. He had stolen it during the looting of Singapore. He didn't remember who from. He had looted so much. He smiled at an idea: perhaps he had stolen it from Davies. He marched towards the condemned man.

"Faster, faster," he snapped, "Hurry."

Davies lifted his head and lowered his spade. His face was black and greasy. His ragged shirt hung from his torn slacks. He looked at Sakamura and did not know him. He had been thinking about a winding country lane outside a Welsh village. The picture was vivid in his mind. . . .

He had come home late from school and he was hurrying, because his mother worried when he was late. It was a hot day and he was panting and sweating. . . .

Then he came back to reality. He panted and sweated. He felt hot, thirsty and uncomfortable. He saw Sakamura. He knew he ought to hate the Captain for all the brutality he had inflicted in the past three years. But he could feel nothing, save the desire to dig, faster and faster. As he dug a picture of his mother came into his mind. But it suddenly evaporated as quickly as it appeared and all he saw was the gaping hole beneath him. He heard more voices and he looked up. He saw that Sakamura had moved over to the machine-gunners, pulling a sword from its scabbard as he did so. For one moment Davies thought the Captain was going to execute the gunners. Then he saw that they were laughing and talking all at once. He couldn't quite understand what was going on. But when he saw the sword raised in the air he stiffened.

The gesture brought back memories of military parades. His mind went back into the past . . . when he wore a smart uniform and carried a similar sword. He stood to attention, placing his spade on his shoulder.

The sun glinted on steel as Sakamura's sword flashed earthwards and the machine-gunners fired a long, steady burst. Davies was still clutching his spade when the bullets cut him down into his grave.

Chapter Two

I

Father Paul Anjou heard the gunfire and closed his eyes, his lips moving in prayer. The noise made him shudder slightly. But he did not open his eyes until his lips had finished the prayer.

On his right stood a Dutch planter, Piet van Elst. Once van Elst had owned the house in which Colonel Yamamitsu nightly fornicated. Van Elst had loved that house he had built with his own hands. He had once loved the surrounding jungle. But no longer.

Only one man in the line-up seemed unmoved by the execution.

On the priest's left, Colonel Lambert, the prisoners' commanding officer, witnessed the murder without emotion. Some men had sworn. Others had crossed themselves. Some had shown fear, others hatred or defiance. A few—very few—showed compassion. But Lambert looked on impassively, objectively, carefully. He missed nothing. He looked at the faces of the three gunners taking a mental note of their features, heights and weights. It was very important that he should remember them.

As they fired that long, steady burst, he made no move; not even his eyes flickered.

Among the line somewhere, a prisoner screamed. Others dragged him back into line as a sentry lifted a sub-machine-gun.

"Order, order," he yelled.

"Dirty bastards," somebody shouted.

"Silence!" screamed the guards.

"Go screw yourselves," another prisoner shouted. "You yellow dingos."

The machine-gun fire died away. Sakamura, his sword back in its scabbard, came hurrying through the camp gates. He snapped orders at his N.C.O.s and the guards moved *en masse* towards the line of prisoners.

Lambert watched one of the N.C.O.s. As he approached, some of the prisoners cowed and began to fall back. The Japanese was a small, squat man. He wore glasses which heavily magnified his eyes. He had a wide mouth, and his facial skin hung in folds. His head was in the shape of a squashed lemon. Once, long ago, the prisoners had called him Lemon Head. But that was in the past, when they had taken an interest in such things and before they had lost their sense of humour.

Lemon Head was impatient and his legs were stumpy and couldn't carry him quickly enough. He started to rap out orders in a flat unmusical sort of voice.

"Grave party move. At once!"

A small group of men shuffled forward.

"Now working parties. Quickly!"

More groups of men moved, but this time rather quicker, as the guards were among them, using rifle butts and heavy sticks.

Only Colonel Lambert refused to move. He half turned and looked at Yamamitsu's bungalow. The Colonel was no longer on the verandah. Lambert sighed. He knew what he had to do, and knew that it was a waste of time. And that almost certainly it would be painful. He had to, as senior officer, make a formal protest against the execution. The Colonel would expect such a protest. So would his Captain. So would the guards, and the prisoners. Lambert's protests had become the Grand Finale to each special execution.

Now, if he did not make one, it would cause speculation. And at all costs, nobody, least of all the Japanese, could be allowed to speculate, to think, suspect. If Yamamitsu became suspicious everything would be lost.

2

The prisoners were all moving off. A party of men, with Father Anjou at their head, went through the prison gates. They moved sluggishly and many limped. Though they had neither the mental courage or physical strength left to offer any resistance, a machine-gunner in the gate tower still trained his weapon on them.

Colonel Lambert was about to head for the bungalow when a small man with grey hair and bright angry eyes snatched at his sleeve.

"Hullo, Beattie." Lambert sounded suddenly weary.

Beattie gestured angrily. "I want you to know, Lambert, that I hold you responsible for the death of Davies."

Lambert looked away from Beattie, his gaze lifting across the wire fence to the shambling grave party. His jaw muscles stiffened.

"That's a strange thing to say, Mr. Beattie." Lambert's voice was firm, but low. "That seems to suggest that I am working with the Japanese. That I, not Yamamitsu, sentenced him. That it was I, not Sakamura who carried out the sentence."

"Don't bandy words with me," Beattie snapped. "If he had not been working for you, Davies would not have died. I hold you responsible. And I will hold you responsible for Doctor Keiller's death, when they capture and execute him too."

"They'll never catch him. He has been gone too long. He must be off this place by now."

"How do you know?" Beattie demanded.

"I don't know for a hundred per cent——"

"There you are. They might have caught him and killed him and kept it from you."

Lambert frowned.

Beattie saw that he was worried. It gave him confidence. He pointed a finger at the Colonel's chest. "You know there is no chance of getting off this God-forsaken island, Lambert." Beattie was almost hysterical. "Has anybody ever got away? Yet you ordered him to escape. Ordered him to die. You are as much a murderer as these bloody Japs."

Lambert, said, still in his soft, level voice, "Control yourself. You're attracting attention."

Beattie looked about him nervously, hoping that the Japanese had not noticed. If they had, and were interested in what they were arguing about, then it could mean torture. Beattie couldn't stand the thought of that. He knew too that the lives of his wife and child, imprisoned in the women's camp, would be at stake.

Lambert reasoned, "I don't think they have caught or killed Keiller. If they had they would have told us. Why should they keep it quiet? No, I am sure they would have told us. It would be a good opportunity to gloat over us."

"All right, all right," Beattie hissed. "He isn't dead. Maybe they haven't caught him. But it is only a matter of time. You ordered him——"

"Shut up and listen, damn you, man. Nobody ordered him to do anything," Lambert said, looking over Beattie's shoulder. "Look out, Sakamura's coming. No, don't turn."

Lambert saw the Captain striding towards them. He looked as if he meant business. Lambert realised that he and Beattie were alone in the compound and that they had attracted attention. Sakamura would demand to know what the camp leader and the former senior diplomatic official of the Colonial Office were arguing about.

Lambert raised his voice. "I'm sorry, Beattie. I cannot worry the Colonel with such trivial matters. You, as hut leader, must decide for yourself."

Beattie took his cue and rasped, "I'm asking you to take up the matter. We can't do anything without the proper equipment."

"Manage the best you can, dammit! These insects are nothing new. Use your head, man!"

"If we move everything from the hut we might kill a few thousand," Beattie flared. "But within a few days the position will be as bad as ever."

"We've been through all this before," Lambert snapped.

"Good morning!"

"Good riddance!"

Sakamura chuckled. It was a dry throaty noise, devoid of humour, full of rasping undertones. Beattie swung, as if aware of the Japanese for the first time.

"So. The British fight among themselves. Good! That is why your Empire is no more. That is why the Japanese are masters of the East and the Germans will soon be masters of the West. But you, my dear Mr. Beattie, must not led bed bugs worry you. No, you are trained. You must colonise them."

Beattie stepped back a pace. His lower lip quivered in rage. The smile left the Captain's face. It became flushed with anger.

"You forget, excellency. Something very important," he rasped.

"Yes, Captain?" Beattie's voice had a nervous edge to it. "I forget?"

"Yes! Bow to officer of Nippon. At once!"

Beattie bowed from the waist.

"Bow once more."

Beattie bowed once more.

"Very good," Sakamura smirked. "Better than you learn at English school of Eton, yes?"

"Yes, Captain."

There was a pause. Then Sakamura lifted his thick stick and whispered, "Come forward, excellency."

Beattie lifted his hand in a nervous gesture. He approached the wire. But Sakamura indicated the gate, and ordered him outside. The sweat gleamed on Beattie's face. He sensed he might get a beating. Sakamura grinned at him. Slapping his stick in the palm of his hand he whispered, "Run, your excellency."

Beattie ran.

"So nice to see English diplomat run. Most unusual," shouted the captain.

Beattie reached the gate and passed through it at a stumble. Sakamura ordered him to bow again. Beattie bowed.

"Officer of Nippon bows to former English diplomat," mocked Sakamura, bowing. Then he pointed to the machine gun used at the execution and smirked, "Greatly honoured to have former diplomat carry humble Japanese gun back to proper place."

The execution squad, about to dismantle the gun looked up. Sakamura told them to let Beattie carry the gun. The squad roared with laughter at the idea. Beattie hobbled slowly towards the gun. The squad loaded it, none too gently, on to his back. Then, bent almost double, Beattie hobbled towards the compound. His face was crimson, a compound of fatigue and injured pride. He felt that the weight of the gun would break his back and burst his lungs. He heard the breath rasping in and out of his body. He felt a blind anger mounting inside him. For a moment he had a deep desire to fall to the ground, turn the gun and cut down his tormentors. But reason stopped him. He told himself that the mechanism of the gun wasn't known to him; that, in any case, the soldiers had probably removed the firing pin. He also remembered his wife and child and the prospect of not seeing them again was unbearable.

He told himself that he could take it. That he could take anything the Japanese handed out, as long as he, and his family could live. Beattie knew that he was prepared to go to any lengths if he knew he, and his wife and child, would survive. He was even prepared to betray his friends for that.

3

Lambert strode purposefully towards the bungalow. He moved as quickly as his lame leg would allow.

Sakamura saw him and forgot Beattie and the machine-gun. He hurried after Lambert. There was an urgency in his steps that belied the bland look on his face.

4

Dawson and Sykes busied themselves cleaning out the latrines. They were always cleaning out the latrines. Nobody liked them, they liked nobody, not even each other. Both were joined in a common bond of defeatism and the fact that they were born lazy. They spent all their time in the fetid smell of the lavatories. Since the latrines were at the extreme end of the camp, they had a good view of everything going on. Both had been watching the baiting of Beattie. Dawson was short and would have been fat if he had all the food he wanted. He also had a beard. Sykes was large, red-headed, bony and wafer thin.

Dawson said, lazily, "Sakamura's a bastard."

"A dyed in the wool one."

"He's also a son of a bitch."

"A real one."

Dawson demanded. "How do you think Beattie feels?"

"No idea."

"Bloody, I expect."

"I expect so. Hey, look who's calling on the Colonel," said Sykes.

"Who? Winston Churchill?"

"No. Hopalong Cassidy. Our brave senior officer."

"More bloody trouble," said Dawson.

"It could be interesting. One of these days that bastard Lambert will complain once too often. This could be his day."

"Balls. Nothing will happen."

"You're telling me," agreed Sykes. There was boredom in his voice. "I'd give a year of my life to get into the women's camp. Then plenty would happen."

"Quit fooling yourself, brother. You're just all shrivelled up."

The two men carried on their conversation in bored tones, their eyes never moving from the verandah. They didn't stop talking until Sakamura reached it, stepped up on the second step, turned and glowered down on Lambert.

Chapter Three

I

FOR long minutes the men stared at each other. Finally Sakamura, hands on hips, snarled, "You have no right to be here."

The interpreter hurried from the house. The two sentries stepped forward and raised their rifles.

"I wish to see the Colonel," Lambert said calmly.

"So? But the Colonel does not wish to see you," lisped the interpreter.

"Since when do you decide who the Colonel sees? I thought only Captain Sakamura could do that?"

It was an effective move on Lambert's part. He had managed to plant the idea in Sakamura's mind that the interpreter was usurping the Captain's authority.

Sakamura turned to the interpreter and told him to stay silent. Then he swung back to the tight-lipped Lambert.

"English officer realise who is senior here. Good. But all the same. I'm very sorry"—his voice belied his words—"Very sorry. But the commandant does not want you in his house. You smell."

The interpreter grinned and held his nose. The two sentries sneezed loudly. Sakamura nodded appreciatively. He liked his audience to join in prisoner-baiting; an art which had developed to a fine pitch in the three years he had been practising it.

"What you did out there, Captain, was murder. Cold-blooded, brutal murder," snapped Lambert.

For a moment there was silence on the verandah. Then several things happened in a flash. The interpreter stepped back a pace, his face covered with shock, amazement and a trace of bewilderment. The two sentries sprang to either side of Sakamura, their rifles at the ready. Slowly, agonizingly slowly, the Captain moved towards Lambert. He started to curse. Softly at first, but as the seconds slipped by his voice rose to a screeching crescendo. Lambert saw that there was a dangerous glint in his eyes. The spittle dribbling down his chin told him that the glint well might be that of a man temporarily insane.

Then he had no more time to think. Sakamura was standing a

foot from him. Lambert swallowed hard and planted his feet more firmly on the ground. The Captain saw this and nodded his head. Casually he drew his hand back. Lambert's eyes followed it and beads of sweat started to coat his brow. Suddenly Sakamura unleashed his hand. Like a watch spring running down it whipped towards Lambert's face, and, with a crack that could be heard fifty yards away, it lashed across his face.

"You shouldn't have done that, Captain. One day you will have to answer for it," gritted Lambert.

"So? You still insolent." Once more Sakamura side-swiped him with a meaty thump. "Maybe you stay silent now."

Lambert sensed the blood trickling down his face; saw the red smears on the back of Sakamura's hand. His face was numbed. He had an overwhelming desire to massage it, to rub some life back into his injured cheeks and battered nose. But he knew the moment he did, Sakamura would be satisfied.

Lambert braced his feet even more firmly and slowly and quietly told the Captain, "There are rules governing the treatment of prisoners of war, Captain. You have broken them. Firstly by murdering Davies for attempting to escape. Now by striking me."

Sakamura went berserk. He leapt at Lambert. His hands gripped his throat, his teeth gouged at his face. The two men fell to the ground. With a powerful lunge, Lambert forced the Japanese away from him. Sakamura slithered to a stop at the foot of the verandah. He bounded to his feet and with a wild rush lashed out with his boots at Lambert. For almost a minute Sakamura rained kicks on Lambert's body. Then, exhausted, he stepped back and ordered the sentries to take over.

At that moment the interpreter stepped forward, and with an apologetic bow to Sakamura, lisped, "Colonel says he now like to see Lambert."

Sakamura flushed angrily. It was a blow to his pride. He had lost face before Lambert. It was not the first time it had happened. It worried Sakamura. He knew he was the master. He knew he could order Lambert to grovel in the mud; he could be beaten. But he could not break his spirit, short of killing him. Sakamura had long thought about that, but something had always held him back.

He turned to Lambert and whispered, "I will not forget this."

"Neither will I, Captain."

Sakamura turned away.

2

Lambert watched him go and smiled. There was no mirth in it. No relief or even satisfaction. It was an automatic gesture. A slight parting of the lips, a momentary gap between the lower and upper jaws. Then lips and jaws clamped together. But Sakamura would have been worried by the gesture. He would have sensed that it brooked no good for him; he had a way of sensing things like that, he had once told Lambert. That had been long ago when the Captain had tried to win Lambert over to his way of thinking. He had failed miserably. That had been the start of their feud. Watching him walk away, Lambert couldn't help thinking that the Captain looked like a farmyard cock. A cock on the rampage, spoiling for a fight, looking for somebody to bully. There would have to be *somebody* for Sakamura was determined to have immediate vengeance on Lambert. One way would be to assault a prisoner who did not have the courage to face up to him.

"Please, Lambert. You come now. Quickly."

Lambert looked at the interpreter. He had changed from a braggart to almost a polite lackey in a moment. It was one of the things Lambert had never understood about the Japanese. They seemed to have an astonishing ability to change.

"Colonel will see you. But only short time."

Lambert nodded.

The interpreter snapped an order—again the bully—and the sentries stepped aside. Lambert walked past them into the house. His face ached terribly. He found great difficulty in breathing through his nose. He wiped some of the blood away with the sleeve of his faded battledress as he followed the interpreter. In silence they moved along a well-carpeted corridor. Finally they came to a halt before a highly polished wooden door. The interpreter knocked and opened it when a voice barked something in Japanese from behind the door.

He held the door open for Lambert to enter and then carefully closed it, bowing all the time as he retreated into the corridor. Lambert thought it was a masterful performance that must have taken years of arduous practice. Lambert walked into the room, noticing in one quick look, the writing desk, couches, bookcases. On the writing desk a gramophone was playing an aria from *Madame Butterfly*. Then Lambert's attention became riveted on the man sitting on a cushion, cross-legged, on the floor. He thought that Yamamitsu looked faintly ridiculous squatting there like an overfed toad. He was holding a dish of prawns and flicking them into his mouth with chop-sticks. He belched as Lambert bowed briefly to him. Then he stopped eating and reached for a cigarette, smouldering in an ash tray. Lambert noticed that the butt was circled with lip-stick. It made him frown.

"My dear Lambert. You have been in some accident," said Yamamitsu. "You must be more careful."

"It was a small thing. Nothing to disturb you, Colonel."

Yamamitsu smiled oilily at Lambert. "I am so glad to hear that. I have been listening to *Madam Butterfly* and it has enough violence for me. I am a man of peace, my dear Lambert."

Lambert said nothing.

"But this music makes me angry. It is so anti-Japanese. Don't you agree?"

"I didn't come to——"

"Don't argue with me, Lambert." Yamamitsu's voice had taken on a sudden edge. "Whatever you say will be wrong. Because I am right. If I was a prisoner and you the camp commandant you would be right. It is"—he reached for an English simile—"as simple as that."

"Of course."

"Good. So listen to me. This opera"—he indicated the gramophone, now silent—"is very anti-Japanese. It infers that our women are all prostitutes. That is not so." He paused to cram more prawns into his mouth. "I assure you, Lambert, prostitution is a western invention."

Lambert said nothing. He had come to make a formal protest about an execution, not to argue over operas. But Yamamitsu had better have his say first. . . .

"Also, Lambert. Operas like *Madame Butterfly* reveal how brutal the West is. Particularly the Americans. Yes? They take Japanese girls, rape them, then sail away leaving them holding the baby, no?"

"I've no idea——"

"You should!"

"Listen——"

"No, you listen," snapped Yamamitsu. "What I say is true. That is one of the reasons why we attacked Pearl Harbour so unexpectedly. The West, especially America, does not deserve any pity."

Yamamitsu placed the cigarette back in the ash tray. Lambert noticed that it still had traces of lipstick. His eyes went towards a a door, slightly ajar, across the room. He caught a glimpse of a bed. He tried to reason out what it all meant. Clearly there was a woman in the house. That much everybody knew. But little else was known. Some said she was white, others Eurasian. Nobody was sure. For one wild moment Lambert was tempted to walk across and push the door wide open and see if the woman was behind that door.

"Well? What do you want?"

Yamamitsu's words brought him back to reality. Lambert braced himself and took a pace forward. "I have come, as senior officer, to protest against the murder of Lieutenant Davies."

Yamamitsu chewed thoughtfully on a prawn. "You question my authority on this matter?"

"Yes."

"You joke, of course?"

"Far from it." Lambert was unruffled. "I question your authority if you allow atrocities like this morning's. I also question your right to withhold medical supplies and food."

Yamamitsu slammed down the dish of prawns, scattering them over the carpet. In one clean movement he sprang to his feet. He struck Lambert on the face as he moved forward. It was a light blow. More of a warning than a punishment. "Do not question my authority."

"I must. It is my duty to place the facts before you. You are breaking all the rules of humane treatment for prisoners. For instance, as well as supplies, why have you left our mail rotting down on the jetty . . . where the boat dumped it three months ago."

"Lambert, shut up!"

"I must place the facts——"

"So——" Yamamitsu sprang to his desk and snatched a pistol from its holster. He spun round and arm extended, pointed the gun at Lambert's temple. "I will kill you. Now!"

Lambert looked steadily at the man. He saw that his nostrils were flared, that his eyes were black and glazed. He felt a sudden coldness stab at his heart. But he knew he had to go on, it was his only hope. When he could trust himself to speak calmly, he said, "I have not finished yet."

"Stop! I order you to shut up." Yamamitsu's facial muscles were twitching. "Silence!"

Lambert heard the click as the Japanese released the safety catch. There was a long moment of silence. Lambert closed his eyes. But he could still sense the nose of the gun wavering in front of his forehead. He lowered his head and opened his eyes. On the carpet he saw a prawn. It struck him that in a moment he would be as dead as that prawn was. He knew he desperately wanted to live, that he had to live. Because so much depended on it. But he was a soldier and an officer. He had come to protest. Everybody in the camp knew that.

"That is better," Yamamitsu whispered. "You silent now. That is much better."

He lowered the pistol and the tension collapsed with it. "You listen to me, Lambert. I never break the rules of war. And you must never raise your voice to me again. Now I have something to say to you." He walked over to his desk and slipped the gun back into its holster. Then he resumed his squatting on the cushion and went on. "The prisoners are giving too much trouble. We know they cut telephone wires, smashed the radio and attempted to escape. That is bad. That is sabotage. And, Lambert, you know that in any country sabotage is punishable by death in wartime. That is one of the rules the West made long ago.

"But you have come here to protest about Davies. That is your job. It is not much use though, coming to me and saying you protest. Your men have done much damage. That we have punished by beatings and withholding privileges. But Davies tried to escape. Why did he try to escape, Lambert?"

"He did not try to escape."

"Lambert," said Yamamitsu in a tired, bored voice, "Don't lie. He tried to escape! Why? I will tell you. He tried to link up with the enemy in the jungles. He wanted to lead them here. Lambert you might think that is a good thing. But can you blame me for wanting to protect my own interests? I am here to guard you all. If I fail and you escape, I shall, how do you say, face the music. That, Lambert, is one tune I would not like to listen to."

"You will have to one day, Colonel."

"Lambert, you are very stupid. For if that day comes you will not be alive to see it. Neither will the others. But, of course, that will not arise. Because Japan cannot lose the war. We have fought too long in the jungle to lose now. When your armies get too close we will annihilate them."

"Maybe . . . !"

"It is a fact. But that is all in the future. You have come to protest. I refuse to accept your protest. What else did you expect? And I will refuse to accept your protest when we capture Keiller. He will be shot."

"If you catch him——"

"Have no fear, Lambert. Captain Sakamura has thought of a novel twist for his execution. I think you ought to hear it, Lambert. I think it is very clever. It is bound to cause much talk. The good Captain thinks that Keiller's wife should be brought from the women's camp to witness his execution. No doubt she will be rather distressed at her husband's death. Very understandable. But I have found that white women have a truly remarkable ability to recover quickly. I have agreed that Captain Sakamura should be allowed to assist her in her recovery. I think it is rather good, don't you? After all, Sakamura is not really a lady's man. He is usually far too occupied to bother with them. But he tells me that he has had his eyes on her for a long time."

Yamamitsu stopped to gather some of the prawns off the floor and pop them into his mouth. Lambert watched him with something akin to real disgust stamped on his face.

"Of course Keiller's wife would not be my choice, you understand? She is too plump in the wrong places for my liking. And a little too old as well. But Sakamura is quite thrilled with the whole idea. He is almost like a schoolboy about the whole thing. It has given him a new incentive to track down Keiller. You know, Lambert, searching for prisoners is a very dull business. It is a routine matter that calls for little imagination. But Keiller's wife will make all the difference."

"That is the filthiest thing I have ever heard from you yet," grated Lambert.

Yamamitsu shrugged. "You want to protest?"

"You'll hang for this——"

"You think so? I shoot you before that." The Japanese rose to his feet and drawing back his thick lips, spat in Lambert's face. "It is Keiller's fault. He escaped. Nobody asked him to. And what chance has he got? He can't go to Malaya or Burma. All held by us. Soon India will be Japanese. So it is foolish to try to leave here. But Lambert, why do you act so foolishly?

You are a brave man, for an Englishman. You behave and when the war is over you could work for Nippon and keep your head."

"When the war is over, you and Sakamura will lose your heads." Lambert spoke too quickly, intentionally so, for Yamamitsu to grasp what he had said.

"What did you say?"

"I said I'll see that the prisoners won't lose their heads again," lied Lambert.

"Lose their heads?"

"I mean they will not misbehave again."

"Good. If we win the war you will keep your heads. If we lose—you lose." He made a sharp chopping gesture. "Then even though you win, you lose. I see to that."

"That——"

"Go. Go," Yamamitsu shouted, gesturing at the door. He screamed something about bowing, but Lambert had turned to leave. He had almost reached the door when he felt a sudden, violent slam in the back and his feet caved beneath him. He hit the carpet with a dull thud and lay winded for some moments. His breath came in short angry spurts and it crossed his mind that he had been kicked in the back by Yamamitsu. "Must bow at all times to me," he intoned, "otherwise must take action against you."

Outside, Lambert heard the thud of heavy boots along the corridor. Then the two sentries entered the room. They grasped Lambert by the feet and dragged and bumped him along the corridor. Then he was lifted on to his feet. He knew what was coming and knew he could do nothing about it. He sensed the rifle butt approaching him seconds before it slammed against his buttocks and he felt himself hurtling off the verandah. The pain in his buttocks still flamed fiercely before it was joined by another, brought about by his clumsy fall on the hard-baked ground and that too was joined by a third—an acrid choking from the dust which spiralled up around him. It was some time before he could lift himself and hobble off towards his hut.

3

Father Anjou climbed into an old, battered truck. The Roman Catholic priest held his old, well-thumbed prayer book. The clergyman looked sad. Death always had a deeply lasting effect on him. He had tried to look at Death dispassionately. He had tried to reason, with the help of a few learned journals, that it was inevitable; that people expected to die; that in some cases they even came to look forward to it.

He had entered the Roman Catholic Church twenty years before. The years had had little effect on him; he still had a slight stoop which took inches off his six-foot-two frame. The racking cough which he had suddenly developed after he had been ordained had grown a little deeper. So had the furrows on his brow. But otherwise he was still the same sort of man.

In his life he had had a number of subsidiary interests—he hated the word hobbies—that ranged from philosophy to music. He also knew a great deal about fields that were usually far removed from the priesthood. He had studied tropical farming, tropical zoology. He knew something about carpentry, dentistry and boat building. All this had helped to make him an invaluable member of the camp. Even the Japanese respected him, or possibly feared him.

He was a strongly built man, and even the meagre prison diet had had little effect on his strength. He seemed to have a boundless well of it. But it was his face which really commanded attention. He had a powerful aquiline nose and eyes that really fixed people. Drive, enthusiasm, command—all were registered on his proud and rather piercing face. And as he climbed into the truck those characteristics were joined by sadness.

Father Anjou was especially sad as the death had been in the women's camp. And he then found it harder than ever to be detached about such a thing. Yet as he bumped along in the truck, his escort smoking and joking among themselves, he wondered about the matter. He knew little or nothing about most of the women in the camp. They were just names. He saw them, he comforted them when he could, but that was about all. He knew that they needed that comfort above all else; they were always frightened and ill at ease.

They had told him little stories about their lives, hopes, joys and sorrows. He had listened gravely as they had revealed to him the infinite varieties of the human soul. But the stories had been little more than caricatures; they had outlined a person for him, but the words had not clothed that person with flesh and blood. He felt he should do more for them. Many of them were fighting a long and ceaseless battle against lives that were slipping away from them. They were people, after all.

People of flesh and blood, which very often was suffering flesh and blood which he must try to spiritually heal. He tried. But at the back of his mind was the conviction that he was not doing enough.

Nobody else thought that. Least of all the Japanese who had grown increasingly suspicious of the priest. They had come to realise that he might be the carrier that took the news between the male and female compounds.

He was.

Father Anjou had a very effective method. He passed his news on to Mrs. Beattie in Latin, the only woman who could understand the language, during services.

4

Lambert entered the long hut and crossed to the little boarded-off partition which was his room. He took a rag from a food tin containing brackish water and bathed his face. Then he sank down on to the bed. He looked slowly round the room and was disgusted with what he saw. The floor was hard-trampled earth. The bed was of bamboo and matting. He rolled over on to his stomach because his back ached. He was lying there when Beattie found him.

"I have a complaint to make," the colonial official snapped.

"Go away! I've had enough of you for one day."

"Lambert you can't talk to me like that. I ought to be shown the respect that my position has. After all, Lambert, I was——"

"Beattie, if you don't shut up I shall personally see to it that you are silenced——"

"Lambert!" Beattie shouted, deeply shocked. "Are you threatening me?"

"Yes! And it isn't an idle threat either. Man, you are about the biggest bloody pest on this camp. I've just had a set-to with Yam-Yam and you come here with a load of crap to unload——"

"Lambert! How dare you. Damn you, man, that's downright insolence. I've a good mind to report you——"

"Yes, Beattie?" There was a sudden icy calm in Lambert's voice and he slowly raised himself off the bed. Very softly he went on, "You had a good mind to report me? Who to, Beattie? Sakamura? He'd like that wouldn't he, Beattie? He'd like to have you licking his heels. And maybe you would like to as well.

What do you say to that, Beattie. Or could it be that you are more interested in keeping in with Yam-Yam? It's an interesting thought, isn't it, Beattie? And of course you know what would happen to you, don't you? There would be a nice little accident. Or maybe not so nice. Some of the prisoners aren't so fussy now as they used to be about killing. . . ."

Lambert's voice died off into silence. Beattie looked at him as if he was seeing a ghost. He swallowed several times and the noise was quite loud in the brittle atmosphere of the room. Then Lambert slowly sank back on to the bed and went on, "Of course, Beattie, you know that I couldn't approve of the men killing you. You know too damned well that I would stand by you. And that's the reason you come here, carping and yapping like some old woman. I'm sick, Beattie, of you and of all you stand for. You've got as much guts as my little finger——"

"Lambert, I came to talk about Keiller, not to be insulted," Beattie's voice had lost its aggressiveness. Now it was almost meek.

"What about him? You've no right to worry over him. You're not even fit to think about him. He has forgotten more about courage than you have ever heard. And for the last time, he was the only man I could send."

"Why?"

"Mind your own bloody business. Who the hell do you think you are coming in here and demanding to know what I do. You're just a bloody professional nosey-parker in civvy street. But you're away from your desk now. You've been away for the past three years. If you want to get back behind it after the war, keep your mouth shut and don't come asking me stupid questions. You get me, Beattie?"

"Y-es. Y-es, I get you, Lambert. And after the war I'm going to make it my job to see that you are properly got for all you have done here. You're worse than the Japs——"

In one lightning movement Lambert threw the food tin of brackish water in Beattie's face.

"Lambert! You're mad, stark, raving mad——"

Lambert hit him then. A light back-handed slap across the face. Beattie recoiled and screamed, "I'll call the guards! I'll tell them what you're planning. Think I don't know——"

Lambert grabbed him around the throat and half choked him. "Shut up, you stupid bastard. You'll get us both hurt."

"Let go of my neck, Lambert. Please, let go," Beattie panted. "You're choking me, choking me. . . ."

Lambert gave his neck one last savage squeeze before pulling his hands away. Beattie sank slowly on to the floor, coughing all the time.

"I'm sorry, Beattie. I lost my temper." Lambert suddenly felt weary of the whole business. "It must have been my row with Yam-Yam that shook me up."

"You're a fool, Lambert. You don't see anybody's point of view except your own. I've got my wife and child here. If anything happens to me, they are on their own. Lambert, you don't even know what that begins to mean to me. Your family are in England. Do you think I want to step out of line in my position?"

"Beattie, I'm not asking you to do anything. All I want is for you to stop riding on my neck about things which are out of your province."

"But Keiller. He's got a wife here. How do you think Kate Keiller feels?"

Lambert frowned and his thoughts went back over the years. He was still frowning when Beattie stomped out. Lambert's thoughts were thousands of miles away—in England and an English spring.

Chapter Four

I

MALA had been waiting for some little while for Captain Sakala, the deputy commandant of the women's camp and answerable only to Colonel Yamamitsu. She had gone to her accustomed place behind a grassy bank partially protected by the stubs of four trees—the trees that had been used for firewood long before. Sakala had brought her there some months before when he had taken an interest in her. As she waited for him she was still unable to decide what she liked most about Sakala: his caresses or the bars of Red Cross chocolate he brought.

As she lay and waited the noises of the jungle were all around her. The rustlings, the whispers, the sudden crackle of twigs.

Mala wasn't a pretty girl. Her nose was too squat and her mouth too big for that. But she had a well proportioned body and she had long learnt how to use her body for bartering. She was a half-caste. Her mother had been Chinese. Her father had either been a tall Swede with a stutter, a Welsh sailor with a squint or an English salesman from Ipswich. Her mother was never sure which. But she had told Mala glowing stories about them all and Mala had come to look upon all three as her father. But that had not made her lot any easier with the other women prisoners. Many of them, she knew, suspected that Sakala was her lover. They had said nothing, but hints had been dropped when she was around; hints about retribution after the war against anybody who associated with the enemy. She was thinking about the hints, when there was a rustling in the grass. She lifted herself, her flimsy, threadbare kimono tightening against her breasts and thighs. She felt a sudden thrill of expectation course through her body as she looked up into the smiling face of Captain Sakala, standing over her and already unbuckling the belt of his trousers.

He was a runty kid in his late teens. He had had little schooling but had learnt how to survive in the gutters of Tokyo. When he had joined the Imperial Army he had risen rapidly through the ranks.

"You bow, yes?" He joked. "Everybody must bow to officers of Nippon."

"I bow to officer," she mimicked, bending forward in a squatting position: She felt his hands fumbling at her kimono.

"You are impatient today," she said. It was a mechanical phrase; she used it every time with Sakala. It gave him pleasure; he liked to feel impatient.

"Always impatient. Very good, eh?" He laughed again. A deep, sensuous laugh.

"Always good," she agreed.

He placed his belt, sword and pistol on the grass. Unbuttoning his tunic he took out several bars of chocolate and a tin of condensed milk. He gave them to her, saying "Make you strong. Make you healthy for me." And again that sensuous laugh echoed in the air. He was still laughing as he placed his tunic on the grass and laid down beside Mala. He chuckled appreciatively as she ate the first bar of chocolate. Then he drew closer to her. She took his hand and placed it inside her wrap. She felt his hands searching urgently over her body. All the time she nibbled her chocolate. Then she nibbled no more. For Sakala had unravelled her kimono in a series of urgent tugs and the warm air caressed her body. For a moment they stared at each other. Then Mala caught his arm and forced it across her breasts. For a moment she studied it and then she made a grab at Sakala, pulling him closer and closer towards her.

Afterwards she lay back and ate more of the chocolate. All around her the noises of the jungle ebbed and flowed. It was like an orchestra tuning up. Then a new sound broke in; the groan of an ancient motor engine coming up the hill towards the women's camp.

Captain Sakala knew that the truck held Father Anjou coming to officiate at the funeral. He knew that shortly he would hear the priest intone the burial service in the cemetery a few yards away.

But it did not disturb Sakala, or Mala, still eating the chocolate.

2

The burial ground was similar to the one at the men's camp. The wooden crosses, and there were far too many, were made of roughly shaped pieces of bamboo. Two women, prematurely aged and clad only in threadbare dresses, toiled at the almost prepared grave as the priest stepped from the truck. He nodded briefly to them. Talking was forbidden on such occasions the Japanese had decreed.

Father Anjou walked towards the compound's gates. A sentry opened them and a short procession of women came out. Behind them came the pallbearers, eight women struggling with two coffins. Father Anjou looked at the faces of the women. They were hard, angular faces. They were the faces of women who had long given up wondering what drove them to stay alive in these hellish surroundings. They were the hurried, bereft, grief-torn faces that the priest had seen in Dürer paintings. They were efficient faces, faces that had not seen make-up for a long time, faces full of stubbornness and determination and great unhappiness. About them too was a barren look; they had long grown to live with their very natural desire to have their men with them again. But they had never learnt how to live with the barrenness they felt.

The coffins were long and oblong. They had been fashioned, with a few crude tools, from orange-box wood. When the dampness of the earth got to them, the wood would warp and change its shape.

All around the pitiful cortège, spaced at short intervals, were heavily-armed guards, weapons at the ready. Father Anjou, his prayer book opened and his head bent, took his place at the head of the cortège. When they arrived at the grave—both coffins were going into one to save space—they formed a circle around it. The ever-watchful Japanese formed a wider one. Two women carefully moved to a position where they could watch the priest's face. One was beautiful. Even the ragged clothes, the fatigue and malnutrition had not destroyed the curves and roundness of her body. The other was older in every way. She was Mrs. Beattie.

They stood close together, eyes cast down, but ready to look into the face of Father Anjou when the time came.

That was why they did not notice the soldier staring at them. Or rather staring at the beautiful girl. His eyes had never left her since they had arrived at the grave. He watched her, hawk-eyed, lids half-closed. In Japan, the women had very small breasts, and that was why he was watching the well-bosomed Kate Keiller. She moved unconsciously and he caught a glimpse of her body outlined under the shabby dress. What he saw he liked.

"Service mustn't be long," rapped out an officer. "No need waste time over corpses. Corpses never appreciate it."

A voice from somewhere in the crowd; a thin, humourless voice answered, "Corpses never bow to Japanese officers. Must be very disappointing for you."

But if the officer heard and understood he chose to ignore it. There was a momentary pause and then he ordered the service to begin.

The same thin and humourless voice, not so loud this time, called out: "Start now . . . die . . . now . . . bow now . . . starve now. . . ."

Father Anjou began to read the words of the burial service. As he approached the Latin blessing Mrs. Beattie looked hard at him, fearing that if she did not do so she would miss the message when it came. The others too were watching him and her. They hoped to pick up the meaning of the message before Mrs. Beattie told them later in the huts.

". . . But may possess everlasting joy," chanted the priest, "Through Christ our Lord. . . ."

The assembly murmured, "Amen. . . ."

Then, speaking slowly and carefully in Latin, the priest addressed Mrs. Beattie, "There is no news of Doctor Keiller. He is still free and we must pray that he will remain so. Your husband is also well," he told Mrs. Beattie. "There is no other news, but tell all the women that I pray for them every night. Tell them to have courage, that we shall be freed soon."

The Japanese officer stepped forward, suspicion written over his face. The soldiers lifted their weapons.

Father Anjou raised his hand over the grave as the officer approached and gave the final Blessing. His hand fell to his side. The officer snapped out an order. The guards closed in. They began to hustle the women back to the camp.

The soldier who had watched Kate Keiller, closed towards her, drawn by strong desire. He reached her and gave her a suggestive prod, "Hully please. Evelybody hully." He raised his hand and brought it across Kate Keiller's chest, "Hully, hully, hully. . . ."

Father Anjou saw this and crossed himself. It was a futile gesture but there was nothing else he could do. Then he trudged slowly back to the waiting truck.

The soldier still dogged the heels of Mrs. Keiller. He stepped aside to let her pass through the gate and watch her walk towards her hut. He saw clearly the outline of her buttocks, and the sway of her hips and his eyes glinted. He had just arrived at the camp from Japan and he had never known a white woman. He was barely seventeen and he was impatient to know all that life had to offer. As he stood and watched her go, a plan began to form in his mind. Later that night, he decided, he would know what a white woman was like.

He didn't know about Yamamitsu's offer to Captain Sakamura.

3

It was late afternoon when Mrs. Beattie passed on the news. Mrs. Keiller listened in silence. Then Mrs. Beattie said, suddenly serious, "I saw that young Jap. He looks as if he means trouble for you, Kate."

"I know."

"Be careful then. Arm yourself with some weapon. Keep with a crowd——"

Mrs. Beattie was about to say something more when there was a screech from outside their hut. They both went out and saw that Mala was bending to scoop up a bar of chocolate. Several other women were watching her with ill-disguised contempt. But as she bent another bar slid from the bosom of her kimono. She hurriedly scooped that up.

"Where did you get them from?" somebody screamed.

"Bloody Jap whore!"

"You're full of syphillis," shouted another woman.

"Kill her! Kill her," several chipped in.

Mala, clutching the bars of chocolate, turned and ran for the safety of her hut. Catcalls and abuse followed her. Soon the abuse had given way to planning....

Chapter Five

I

HE lay face down in the kalai grass and pressed his fists to his eyes. But even that couldn't stop the sobs that racked his body.

John Keiller knew that he was coming to the end of his tether. His mind was in a turmoil and he had to fight off a mixed group of visions which threatened to unbalance him completely. One moment he was eating chicken-and-apple pie. Another moment he was in an operating room. Another in an aeroplane flying through great, grey banks of cloud. It made him dizzy, sick and terribly tired.

He had grown more tired every hour that he put between himself and the camp. With the tiredness had come bitterness. He remembered that Lambert had said that he stood as much chance in the jungle as the Japs did. The advantages, Lambert had said, were the same for both. There was fresh water, plenty of cover. It was simply an attitude of mind that lost a man the right to escape in the jungle.

Keiller had believed that when he had made his break for freedom. But from the start things had gone wrong. It had rained all of the first day; a dank, depressing downpour that had dampened his enthusiasm. His meagre supplies had been soaked and had become inedible.

Then he had lost his way. He had headed a little west of north, a course that had taken him uphill slightly. He had soon found that the going had grown more difficult. His pauses for breath came more often. He had been forced to eat grass and roots. As a doctor he knew what was edible and what wasn't. That was one of the reasons why he had been selected to go with Davies and make a dash for help. Lambert had learnt that somewhere on the mainland, in the general direction he was travelling was a native camp. There he hoped to find guides who, for a handsome consideration to be paid later by the British Government, would take him to the guerrillas or to Allied forces.

Lambert had conceived the idea as soon as he had heard that the war had ended.

As Keiller lay there he remembered Lambert saying, "Our

only hope of survival is that we are freed before Yamamitsu knows that it is all over."

The camp committee had heard these words in silence. Then Beattie had spoken out against any action likely to antagonise the Japanese. He had been a lone voice. Urgent plans had been formulated. The upshot had been that hours before Keiller escaped and Davies died at a special execution, the camp's radio station had been sabotaged. The only line of easy communication with the mainland had been severed. The Japanese on Blood-Island could not know that the fighting had ceased.

But as Keiller lay on the ground with great sobs, shaking his body, he wondered if he would reach the native camp in time . . . or if he would ever reach it.

He had been travelling blindly through dense jungle for three long days. At nights he had taken to the trees to sleep fitfully. He had encountered every form of obstacle—vines, bamboo thickets, rattan, atap, scrub, thorn and other natural trip wires. His arms and legs had been badly cut by brambles. His damp clothes had started to rot in the steamy atmosphere. As he moved the cloth chaffed against his buttocks, thighs and chest, making the skin red and very tender. It had become agony to make any sudden movement.

His feet had started to blister under the unaccustomed exercise. The water had made his worn boots feel like two bits of soggy cardboard. His progress had been a nightmare. To start with he had nothing with which to cut a way through the jungle. He had to force and ease his tortured body past obstacles. His compass was an old-fashioned affair, not at all accurate. He had noticed that several times it had taken him in circles. As there were no landmarks, save the tree trunks, which all looked alike after the first hour, he had tried to travel by the sun. But his glimpses of that had been infrequent due to the fact that the trees had matted overhead to form a natural canopy.

It took him over an hour at night to climb up into a tree branch. There he grew steadily colder, for the jungle is a cold place at night. At first light he would thankfully clamber down and search for water. He knew the risks of typhus, but the demand of thirst overrode all else.

Then he would set off once more. As he got deeper into the jungle new hazards had come to try him. There were roars from some animal, the swish of some giant bird skimming the tree tops overhead and always, always the mosquitoes. They bit him everywhere. But worse, from a psychological point of view, was their constant whining about his head. He had quickly found there was something positively ethereal about that humming. He had pawed and lashed at the air. But the moment he stopped the banshee noise had returned again, louder than ever. His eyes had been bitten so badly that they had puffed up and were mere slits in his swollen face. His lips had been lacerated by the insects until they were mere strips of bloody blubber. But even worse than the mosquitoes were the midges.

They were rather bigger than mosquitoes. They did twice as much damage. He had no warning that they were approaching, for their wings beat silently on the air. Then they would swoop; squadrons of them dropping like *Kami-kazi* pilots on to his body. They had a sting that was akin to a bad nettle rash. In minutes they turned his body into a ball of fire.

But still he had pressed on, even though by now he knew he had no chance of surviving. His strength had started to run out. The stops became more frequent. Soon they were coming every few yards. They grew longer. By the third day his progress had been cut down to under a mile a day.

He noticed too, in the detached way of a person looking outside of himself, that his behaviour had become strange. He would laugh and shout for no apparent reason. Several times he told himself that he must be going mad. The idea seemed to please him. He thought that if he was mad there would be no need for him to continue with his mission. Nobody would heed a madman.

But Keiller knew that there was no need for madness to overtake him to stop him going on.

Something far worse had intervened.

A Japanese patrol was beating the jungle about him.

Lambert had said that the advantages were equal in the jungle. That was perfectly true. Except that there were more Japanese ready to take the advantages.

2

Keiller looked about him. On his left was a heap of volcanic boulders heavily bearded with moss. Behind, and to his right were clumps of azalea which merged into thickets of bamboo. The thickets clicked and sighed all the time as the life of the jungle pulsed against them. Keiller had grown used to the pulsing and had come to fear it too. The noise seemed to warn him that he was intruding where he wasn't wanted.

Then he had heard the patrol.

He couldn't remember what had first warned him. It might have been a rustling: a soft swish in the undergrowth that was louder than the noise made by a passing snake. Or it might have been the sudden hostility he sensed in the air and the overpowering feeling that the jungle was closing in on him, that the trees had hunched their leafy heads and were crouching and waiting for something to happen.

For a minute he had to lay there in the green gloom. The strain of going without sleep, the lack of food, the insect bites, all helped to bring his skin out in a deep sweat. His nerves were stretched to breaking point. He started to swear softly. In the past he had found that cursing was a safety valve. But this time it did no good.

"Don't panic," he whispered to himself. "For God's sake keep your head."

He looked about him for a weapon. All he could see were some rotting branches and chips off the boulders. He looked for a way to escape, or a safer place to hide. But the jungle seemed the same wherever he looked. There were salla trees, shiny-leaved azalea, matted vines and the bamboo.

It was the bamboo which had given him the first warning. He had heard the scrape of a body thrusting gently through it. That had been minutes before. Minutes in which his courage had soared and dropped. Minutes in which he had thought of a hundred ideas to outwit the patrol. But in the end he had discarded every idea. Then there had been no more time to think.

For he had heard the voices of the patrol. At first they had been mere whispers that had blended with the noises of the jungle. He had strained to locate them. But they seemed to be all around him. As he had listened they had grown louder with the curious high-pitched tone that voices have when they are still some distance away. At first he had not been able to say how many there were. But as he waited, Keiller was able to pick the individual voices out. He decided there were five. They made little attempt to talk quietly; confident that they had the jungle to themselves save for Keiller. And he would offer little opposition to them, with their guns, grenades and ample supplies.

Keiller heard one of the voices break into a laugh. It startled him. Then the other voices broke into a rapid jabbering.

The patrol had picked up his trail.

Suddenly the jungle went very quiet. In the silence Keiller could hear his own breathing and the thumping of his heart. He pushed his body harder into the ground. But the noise was still too loud. God, he thought, I wish I was fitter. He shifted his foot to a more comfortable position and the noise carried clearly.

"Kali-kali." The voice came from the left, behind the thickets. It was followed by sudden laughter. Then Keiller distinctly heard a Jap say, "Fan out. . . ."

The clamour of the advancing patrol filled the jungle. Keiller could clearly hear them; pushing and shoving their way through the jungle. They *must* get me, he thought, they *can't* miss me. His legs felt suddenly weak and a burning sensation filled the pit of his stomach. Before he knew it, saliva was drooling down his lips. Then he felt a fierce surge of unrest. He wanted to die fighting, if he had to die. And as suddenly as it came, his courage left. And his nerves, already strained well past breaking point, started to twang and hum.

It took him a few seconds to realise that the jungle had grown silent once more. It was an oppressive, stifling, unhealthy silence. Keiller could hear the silence, with its suggestion of movement and its hint of the unexpected. He daren't move.

The sweat was pouring over his body now.

But he daren't move.

The patrol, he knew, were waiting for him to make that one move.

It was going to be a game of cat-and-mouse. They knew there was no way out of the trap. What was worse, Keiller also knew. It only needed a cough, a fractional move, a twitch of an aching muscle for the trap to be sprung.

"Soldier! Stand up!"

The voice was loud and clear. It was about fifty yards from Keiller. It brought on a terrible wave of terror in his tortured mind.

"You cannot escape. Come out, you will die quicker that way."

A burst of laughter rasped through the jungle. It seemed to come from all round Keiller.

Then the silence clamped down.

And the jungle decided to enter the drama. The flies; dragonflies, rainflies, swampflies sought Keiller out with a new vengeance. They didn't come in swarms but in clouds. The clouds hummed angrily over his head and then dropped. Thousands upon thousands settled on every exposed part of his body. They made themselves comfortable and then they bit, and bit in an attempt to relieve their quest for blood. Soon he was a mass of blood.

The jungle knew no pity.

3

For an hour Keiller had lain still. For an hour there had been silence. And in that hour of waiting silence Keiller had suffered every agony of suspense that his imagination could imagine. Every noise had become a whispered command that would have been the prelude to a burst of gunfire directed at him. As he waited he had become convinced that the jungle was biding its time; that like the wheels of railway carriages—with their seeming ability to hammer out a constant message as they turn—the trees were saying time and again to him, "we can wait . . . we will watch them get you . . . we can wait. . . ."

Then he saw him.

4

It was incredible. If he lifted a weakened arm he could have touched him. The Jap was sideways to him. One moment the spot had been empty, the next moment he was standing there after appearing like a wraith from the thick, stifling foliage.

Keiller watched him in agonised fascination. There was a sweat-stained, black-papered cigarette dangling from his mouth. His shirt was open and his sleeves rolled up. The black hair on his chest and arms glistened with sweat. Keiller had an over-all impression that he was looking at something repulsive which had crawled out of the earth.

The Jap carried a sub-machine gun. He held it loosely crooked under his arm, the way a sportsman carries a shot-gun. For a wild, fleeting moment, Keiller had a vision of a fox-hunt. He was the fox and a few yards away was a hound. The man looked carefully about him. It was a lazy and bored sweep of the eyes. Then he relaxed and lowered his gun.

Keiller held his breath.

It was fantastic that the man had not seen him. Then Keiller realised why. The man wasn't really looking for him at that moment. He was looking for a spot to relieve himself. The Jap was an egotistical man, particular where he dropped his waste. He carefully placed his sub-machine-gun on the ground and moved away to a fold in the ground a few feet farther on, undoing his belt as he moved.

Before he reached there Keiller had made his mind up. It was not a conscious reaction, rather the reflex movement of a once-disciplined mind. He had started to inch his way forward before he knew he was doing so. Then he had the gun in his hand. In a split-second he had reversed it. The ugly, squat barrel was trained on the Jap, who, sensing something amiss, swung round.

His arms flashed up. He cringed back. His trousers fell down.

Keiller pressed the trigger. It was a savage, violent movement. The gesture of a man determined to wreak as much pain and havoc as possible.

Nothing happened.

Keiller felt the sweat oozing down his face. His eyes smarted with the liquid. It dripped down his cheek like a stream.

The Jap recovered. He moved forward and tried to break into a run. But his trousers, around his boots, hampered him.

Keiller pressed the trigger again. And again nothing happened. His shaking hand slid along the trigger guard, seeking the safety catch. He didn't know the make of the weapon. Or whether it had a safety catch.

The Jap hobbled forward, shouting and cursing all the time. "*Tennu-heiki. Banzai! Tennu-heiki!*"

From behind him, Keiller heard an answering shout, followed by a wild trampling through the jungle. Keiller looked up. The Jap was a few feet away. He was crouched to spring. Keiller's hand lodged on a clip. He tugged at it, pressing the trigger as he did so.

The gun stuttered into life. The jarring shook Keiller to his core, and the weapon nearly danced out of his hands. He saw the flame spurting from the muzzle and it gave him a feeling of power. He swung the gun in a wide arc and a bright fan of tracer peppered the trees.

The Jap jack-knifed forward with a choked gurgle. For a

moment he stopped in that position, coughing out blood. Then he gave a final gurgle and dropped to the ground like a broken puppet.

"Hannoi-hai! Hannoi-hai!"

Keiller spun round and fired another burst at the voices coming up fast behind him. It was a wild, inaccurate burst that did no damage. But it sent new life surging through his body.

He broke into a trot and thrashed his way through the lush, clinging, stifling foliage. He moved for what seemed like ages, the excitement keeping his leaden limbs moving. Behind him he heard a sudden cacaphony of voices. He looked over his shoulder and saw nothing but the path he had pioneered through the jungle.

But he knew what had happened. The rest of the patrol had found their comrade. Their voices were angry. But Keiller could detect a certain amount of new respect in them. A man with a gun was a different proposition.

Then he heard them crashing after him.

The noise gave added impetus to his flight. God, he had to live! Please God, he prayed, don't let them! They would kill him. That would not be so bad. But it would be the method of the killing. They might use him for bayonet practice; slicing their blades through his emaciated flesh. It would be horrible.

He knew it wouldn't be long before they caught up with him. They had only to follow the track he had made through the jungle. The going was tough for him, because he had to break his own path. But all the patrol had to do was to dog his footsteps.

It took them an hour to do that. They had suffered somewhat doing so. Their uniforms had been stained black with sweat and stuck to their aching bodies. They were out of breath and unprepared for a long fight.

But Keiller was.

They came upon him in a clearing and Keiller was effectively sheltered in a hollow.

Keiller knew that death was very near. But he welcomed it. After all he had suffered it was something to look forward to. But he was going to sell his life dearly. He had decided on that the moment he had burst into the clearing and saw the hollow.

For minutes he had crouched there and looked about him. He could see little, for the day was closing. He settled the butt of the sub-machine-gun more comfortably in the hollow of his armpit and looked back the way he had come.

"Come on, you bastards," he breathed. "Come on and sample some of this medicine...."

They came on.

Then they stopped. Keiller guessed they were very near and were casting round for a way to approach him without any risk of getting shot. He shifted and swung the gun in a narrow arc that covered ten yards of jungle on either side of the path he had swathed. The movement sent some dust seeping up around him, enveloping him, making him look like some phantom from another world.

His movements became slow and precise. He lay the spare clips of ammunition (he had picked them up when he had grabbed the gun and stuffed them into his pocket) by him, then checked the mechanism of the gun so that he was completely familiar with its working.

He could hear the patrol creeping forward. There were short rustlings; the slither of boots inching over a grass carpet.

"Come on, you bastards, I'll take some of you with me," murmured Keiller, lifting the gun an inch. He thought of Kate and he felt a surge of emotion course through his body. He would never see her again, never speak to her, never hear her voice, touch her lips with his, see the laughter light her face.

Then he saw the first Jap. He was about thirty feet away, hugging the trunk of a bala tree. He was a moon-faced man, with high cheekbones. That's all Keiller had time for. The Jap had dropped to cover. Keiller wasn't worried. The patrol would have to come to the edge of the clearing if they were to get him. And then he would be ready.

The daylight had almost gone, when the curtain finally went up. Two Japs stepped boldly into the clearing. There was a tall one with a diamond-shaped face, and a tubby one, who looked like an advertisement for a brand of car tyre. They were half-way across the clearing when they hesitated. They were about to drop to cover when Keiller rose from the hollow. He came up on his knees, his face masked in sweat.

"Come on, you bastards," he screamed, firing as he spoke. "Here's a bloody message for your Emperor."

The first burst took the tubby man in the face. His chin disintegrated. Keiller hit the tall man as he was falling to the ground. He zipped him up the middle with a burst of fire and his stomach and chest opened like a waistcoat shedding its buttons.

There was silence. It weighed heavily in the air. Even the animal life had stopped.

A high-pitched voice broke it. In broken English it yelled:

"Give up. We fixi-fixi you now. Good and properly."

"Bollocks!"

"We give you quick death you come out now."

"I said, 'Bollocks!' "

Once again the silence returned. Keiller could hear an odd whisper, but no more. He sensed what they would do: circle him, mow him down from all sides.

Then the voice rent the air again:

"You come now. All fine. I count ten. Then we come get you. You suffer much then. . . ."

Silence once more. But only for a moment. The voice started counting.

"*Ichi!*"

Keiller fired three rounds at where he thought the voice came from.

"*Ni!*"

He fired another burst. Longer this time. But the counting went on.

He was still undecided what to do when all hell broke loose. Bullets stapled a pattern around him, hit and bounced off the ground, buzzed angrily through the air. He fired back. Burst after burst.

Then his ammunition ran out.

He realised it too late. He hadn't even saved a bullet for himself. The Japs strode towards him, laughing and shooting over his head.

They stood around the hollow, looking him over. There were three of them. They looked at each other for a few moments; the white man and the yellow; the brave and the bullies.

Keiller laughed at them. He was still laughing when they hauled him to his feet, tearing his clothes from him, so that they could beat him better with the butts of their guns.

He was still laughing when he lapsed into unconsciousness.

Chapter Six

I

NOBODY could say exactly where the rumour started. A number said that Dawson and Sykes had started it during an idle moment in their latrine duties. Dawson and Sykes denied this. They insisted that Solman had told them.

Solman was the self-appointed camp psychologist. Nobody ever consulted him. But he offered deep psychological reasons for anything and everything that happened in the camp. Life today, he preached, was incredibly complicated. Most of the prisoners retorted that the only complications were the Japanese. Solman would ignore that point or, if forced to debate it, would say that the guards were only a symbol of something far deeper. When he had reached that stage there was no holding him back. Pleas to shut his mouth, threats that if he didn't somebody would shut it for him, and cajoling were brushed aside. Nothing was easy, he would say; work demanded more effort and play was not easy (everybody agreed about those two points). Thinking can be painful and even love was often a torment rather than a joy. Nobody had ever quite understood what Solman was getting at there.

Yet in many ways he was uniquely qualified to talk on psychology. For twenty-two years before his capture he had been concerned with the mental health of the Singapore public. He had worked in a mental hospital there and had later transferred to a psychiatric clinic and for two years before his capture had been employed by the public health service of the island.

Solman had been a general handyman all his life.

He had learnt his psychology from text-books borrowed from a variety of sources. And in between sweeping out wards and offices, Solman had come to love the technical language of Freud, Wagner and the other doctors of the mind. It had been like learning a new language for him. He had mastered the basic rudiments at first; the commonplace phrases "nerves" and mental breakdown." After that he had rapidly developed, and was soon able to sprinkle his conversation with such words as "nervosa anoxia", "manifested delusions", "depressive mania."

Somewhere in his studies somebody dubbed him as The Man Who Knew Too Much. It was a tag which stuck, and Solman, with all his studying couldn't see why. He refused to accept the answer when he saw it in a text-book under the chapter heading of Inferiority Complex. Solman was a small man physically. He could do little about that. So he had armed himself with mental stilts to walk through life. His passion for psychology was to make him feel superior to his surroundings. It had also made him a bore.

But Solman was not so desperate for company that he would have started the rumour that Keiller had got through and that the Allies were on the way to liberate Blood Island. He knew that if he had started it and it had proved wrong he would have had short shrift from the other prisoners.

All the same the rumour provided him with an interesting psychological problem. A problem which he could talk over with his only friend. Doctor Horace Smith. Horace wasn't a doctor in the accepted sense, though he held a number of degrees, all bogus. Horace had been a travelling salesman peddling quack cures when the Japanese had caught him in Malaya. He was a small, tubby, jovial man who had accepted his fate without a qualm. He told astonishing stories of his adventures, none of which were believed. Inevitably he had been drawn towards Solman. They had a bond: they could discuss how the mind and body could work together. From their vast store of unrecognised authority they would discuss how other prisoners could adapt the psychological equipment of Life to their own needs.

Horace was sitting on his bed when Solman cornered him about the rumour.

"It might well be true," said Horace knowingly. "On the other hand it might not," he said equally knowingly. Horace had always found a careful, non-committal approach to life had served him well.

"The mental strain must have been great in the jungle," said Solman. "It is a well known fact that it is easy to develop claustrophobia under those conditions."

"Is that so?" Horace wasn't quite sure what claustrophobia was; he had a feeling it might be an offshoot of the chlorophyll tablet racket.

"Of course, he must have suffered from an acute state of anxiety. . . ."

2

By the time the rumour had reached Watkins it had grown respectably: Keiller had got through, ambushing and killing a platoon of Japanese on the way. He had rounded up a small army of guerrillas and a few platoons from the advancing 5th Army and was at their head about a day's march from Blood Island.

"I don't bloody well believe it," said Watkins. He never believed anything. Before being captured he had been in the pawn-broking business.

He was in a minority.

3

"Knackers" Jenkins believed it unquestionably. He believed anything and everything. He mulled the rumour over for a few minutes and decided it needed strengthening a little. When he passed it on to "Nobby" Clarke he added that Keiller's ground forces—everybody somehow assumed that Keiller was in command—were being backed by an air armada.

"What the hell are they going to do from up there?" Clarke was a suspicious man. He had been a ledger clerk during the years leading up to the fall of Singapore. He had been suspicious of the books he ledgered, and that suspicion had followed him into private life. Soon it had become an established part of his life. People regarded him as shrewd.

"What do you think they'll do up there? Come on down and give the Japs hell!"

"What about us? We might get hit too!"

"Knackers" mulled that over for a few more minutes. There had to be a way to cover the flaw.

"They'll give us a warning."

"How?"

"That's secret."

"Why?"

"Chrissake! How should I know?" Jenkins could see that his elaboration was not so air-tight after all. "I don't make the rules."

"No. But hell, man, can't you see what it means if they bomb this place. We'll be blown to bits as well."

"I know. That's what worries me."

The two men were silent for a few minutes. Then "Knackers"—he earned his nickname for the years he'd worked in a glue factory—brightened and said:

"You're wrong, Nobby. Nobody said they were coming to bomb this place. I didn't anyway. No, the whole thing is far slicker than that. They're going to drop parachutists on the camp. These bloody Japs won't know what hit them."

"Parachutists, eh . . . ?"

"Knackers" nodded emphatically. The flaw had been removed. He felt almost happy.

"Could be you're right, 'Knackers'. It could well be. . ."

4

Parsons discarded the idea of parachutists as soon as he heard it. He was a hulk of a man, a soldier of fortune who had left his native Belfast thirty years before to fight on whatever side paid the most. The idea of somebody else coming to do the fighting on his behalf left a flat taste in his mouth.

"There just ain't a word of truth in it. Mon, can't you see that it isn't going to be so?" he bellowed at Adams, a soldier, who had passed the rumour on to Parsons.

"If you say so, Pat."

Adams couldn't care less. All his life he had either accepted or passed on rumours without elaboration. He was a sort of human post-bag.

"No, mon. They're going to parachute arms down to us."

"Is that so?"

"Sure it is, Adams. And just give me a bloody Tommy-gun in ma hands and then watch those Japs totter."

Parsons dropped to one knee and swung his arms in a wide circle, making a stuttering noise as he did so.

5

Archer was the first who tried to kill the rumour. In slow, matter-of-fact tones he said to the rest of his hut, "I ask you, gentlemen, consider what it means to us."

There was silence in the hut. John Foster Archer was a man to be listened to with great respect. Before the war he had been one of the most eminent King's Counsel at the English Bar. He had brought to the criminal bar the rare combination of simple eloquence and skilled forensic thought. At one stage he had been the real, though not the titular, head of the active criminal bar. He had been defending in a case on the island when Singapore fell. The little man—he was 5 ft. 6 in. of controlled logic—had been brought to Blood Island along with scores of others. His indomitable spirit had kept him going when others had fallen by the wayside. At fifty he was as fit as many men half his age.

For nearly twenty years he had differed diffidently with judges of every kind from the rarefied heights of the High Court to the barren depths of Land Tribunals. He had learnt his art as counsel in divorce actions, breach-of-promise cases and other kinds of litigation. But he was not a specialist. He once had said he specialised in advocacy.

"I ask you, gentlemen, have you realised what it would mean to us if this story were true?"

"What, sir?" a voice demanded.

He looked round at his audience, as in the past he had looked round the courtrooms of England. His eyes blinked furiously. His narrow lips parted in a friendly smile. His mouth hung open for several seconds. Even without his wig and gown he looked the part of a barrister.

"It means this. Simply this. And no more." He might have been making a closing speech. "It means we will all die before any help from the outside can be effective. Gentlemen, that is the position. For the moment I will only say that."

He was no Marshall-Hall with the thunderous voice. He had no gold pencil like a Birkett to mesmerise a witness. He had none of the pungent Irish wit that Edward Carson had. But he had caught the undivided attention of every man in his hut. Now he was prepared to go on.

"Gentlemen." His voice had the quiet authority he had used when addressing a Judge on a point of order. "Let us examine the situation at this moment. Let us look at it in its proper perspective. Devoid of embellishment. Let us seek the truth of this rumour."

He smiled. It was a thin and humourless smile. It was a smile that spoke far louder than any words. It told his listeners that John Foster Archer, K.C., just did not believe the story.

"Who," he began, "started this story? Who can say without a doubt that it is true? Gentlemen, can you answer that? Can any of you stand up and tell me that you know for a fact that all the stories, or even one of them, have a grain of truth? Can you?"

There was an uncomfortable silence. Then a thin voice broke it with:

"But the whole camp is talking about the rescue, sir!"

"Y-yes. I see. And because everybody is talking about it, you believe it. A most interesting state of mind. Most interesting. But utterly impossible to deal with this position. Examine the facts! They are few and far between. Keiller has escaped from the camp. The Japanese have gone after him," Archer raised his hands in supplication. "And that is all we know. The rest is invention. And invention has no place in a situation like this. It is far too serious. Does anybody still think that we are going to be suddenly and dramatically snatched away from under the noses of our captors? Well, gentlemen?"

There was silence in the hut.

"I guess you're right, sir." The thin voice spoke for all the listeners.

6

Lambert finally killed the rumour. Beattie came to him and asked if it was true. Lambert said he didn't think so. It was the way he said it that mattered.

"So he's dead?"

"How should I know, Beattie?"

"You don't care, either!"

"Beattie, if you say another word I'll beat your brains in."

Beattie grunted and stalked off. Within minutes he had started the rumour that Keiller had died minutes after leaving the camp.

Dawson and Sykes thought it was a lot of crap. Watkins refused to believe a word. "Knackers" Jenkins believed it. So did Adams. Parsons swore and his dream of doing an Errol Flynn collapsed.

The rest shrugged their shoulders.

Chapter Seven

I

THEY shrugged until they heard that Sakamura was seeking revenge for his loss of face with Lambert. They received the news with various reactions. Some took to their huts. Others vanished into the latrines. A few decided that the best way to avoid Sakamura was to keep a careful eye on him at a respectable distance.

It made no difference. Captain Sakamura had selected his victim long before the prisoners knew that he sought one.

His choice was Arthur Sheppey, the quietest man on the camp.

Sakamura was pleased with his choice. For three years he had tried to find an excuse to humiliate Sheppey. He knew he could have done so without an excuse. But it gave him more satisfaction to have one. It was one of the strange facets of his personality.

2

Arthur Sheppey had been the science master at Singapore High School. He was a sweaty little man, neutral and nondescript. He had watery brown eyes that blinked behind thick horn-rimmed spectacles, a thin, narrow face with an unusually determined chin that jutted out above his thin body.

He had been born in Wandsworth, London, fifty-three years before. He still had a trace of the accent peculiar to that borough; a faint lisping, a guttural way of rolling r's; he had also developed a trick of making even a simple statement sound like a question.

Sheppey had graduated from the University of London with a B.Sc. Honours. His mother had framed his diploma, and as far as he knew it still hung in her two-up and two-down terraced house in Wandsworth.

He had gone East in 1930. The Great Slump, with the advent of national unemployment that was reminiscent of the eighteenth century, had driven him away from Britain. Sheppey liked security. There was a glut of schoolteachers, all with degrees that overnight had become worth nothing more than the paper they were mass-produced on.

With him had gone his newly-won bride, Mandy—a rather romantic name for a tall, severe and angular woman who had also taught science until Sheppey had proposed to her. She had accepted with alacrity. It had been her only proposal. She was twenty-seven well preserved years old when they had married. It had been a quiet wedding. Sheppey hated fuss.

They had settled down happily in Singapore, despite the snobbishness of the Club set. As Sheppey was not a clubman, this bothered neither of them. They had lived soberly in a neat little detached house in a quiet suburb. Then tragedy had struck savagely. Mandy had caught a chill. In a few hours it had turned to pneumonia. Mandy had died in two days.

Sheppey had buried her quietly and without fuss. Then he had gone back to his teaching. People marvelled how well he took the tragedy. Nobody guessed at the suffering that went on inside his mind.

Only his pupils noticed the change in him. His clipped humour which he kept under careful lock and key slowly became locked away for ever. He became moody and depressed. He found fault easily with their work.

Inevitably they found a nickname for him. They called him the Little Sod.

Sheppey soon lived up to his nickname.

When the war came many of his students almost welcomed the Japanese. It meant that for a while there would be no more school. And no more Sheppey. He had been in his laboratory when the Japanese had surrounded the school. A platoon had burst in to the science room and with childish delight had wrecked everything in sight. A burst of gunfire had damaged the gas system that lit the Bunsen burners. In minutes the laboratory had been well alight. Sheppey had been dragged to safety by the patrol. But once they had got him in the open the soldiers had ruthlessly beaten him, shouting all the while that he had been responsible for destroying the laboratory. Then he had been shut up in Changi Jail along with the others: Russell Braddon, Colonel Mackenzie, whose daughter was one day to be a famous television star, Piet Williams, who was to get a M.C. for his bravery during the fight for Singapore, and many others too.

Sheppey came to know them all and they to know him. And when he left for Blood Island their lasting memory of him was of a little man with a desire for peace and quiet. That desire had not left him when he had arrived on Blood Island. He troubled nobody and nobody troubled him over much, save the odd guard who had none-too-gently beaten him with the flat side of a bayonet.

Sheppey spent most of his time on his bed. He either sat there or lay there, dreaming all the time of the past. He not so much dreamt, but relived what he had done, especially what he and Mandy had done.

He was thinking of Mandy when he became aware that Sakamura was looking down on him.

"Well, well, well, little man," purred Sakamura, "what are you doing?"

"Nothing, sir."

"Nothing?"

Sakamura took a pace forward and deliberately slashed his hand across Sheppey's face. "You should be doing something. You should be bowing at me. Don't you know that?" Before Sheppey could move Sakamura lashed him again across the face. "Bow, little man, bow!"

Sheppey scrambled to his feet and bowed. As he bent forward, Sakamura rabbited him in the nape of the neck. Sheppey dropped to the ground like a log.

Sakamura smiled, kicked the inert man once on the side of the head, and walked out of the hut. He would be back. His fun had only just started.

Outside the dusk was falling.

It fell over Lambert watching the working parties returning to the camp.

It fell over Beattie watching Lambert.

It fell over the women's camp. Over Mala, cringing in her hut, knowing that she had been found out, knowing too that her lover could not be with her all the time, that it would be so easy for the women to strike her down. It fell over Beattie's wife. It fell over Kate Keiller, a fear-crazed woman, wondering about her husband, wondering when the young soldier would come and rape her. She sensed it would happen that night. He would come when the hut was quiet. He would be armed. He would prod her and order her outside. At gun-point he would take her to the grass. From there it would be useless to protest. She knew the whole sordid routine from a score of other women who had gone through it. Their advice had been; don't struggle. It only makes them more passionate and more hurtful. Kate wondered how hurtful it would all be. Her husband had been a gentle lover. He had been her only lover.

It fell over Keiller, laughing into unconsciousness in the jungle.

By the time Sakamura had reached the camp gates the daylight was reduced to a mere glimmer. In that glimmer Sakamura looked positively evil. He was thinking out the finishing touches to what he would do with Sheppey.

3

Lambert watched the working parties straggle into line-up. They drooped, were gaunt, fatigued, half-starved. But Lambert insisted on the nightly line-up, like he insisted on a lot of things that the men couldn't understand.

Dawson, watching from the door of the latrines, with Sykes said, "Limpy Lambert is a bloody hard man."

"He's the Captain Bligh of Blood Island," said Sykes in a moment of inspiration.

"That's good. Really good. That just about sums the man up."

The line-up was ready. A man who had once been big and fat and who wore the tattered uniform of a R.S.M. stepped forward. His skin hung loosely beneath his chin like a scarf. He limped over to where Lambert stood. As he did so the Japanese guards moved off to their own quarters for chop suey. The R.S.M. saluted. It was quite a smart salute, for tradition and training die hard in such a man. Dawson had nicknamed him The Goon.

"Working party all present, sir."

"Thank you sargnmajor. Dismiss them."

The R.S.M. hesitated for a moment. Then he took two paces forward. "Beg pardon, sir, but there's a lot more of the men limping tonight. It was a swine out there today, sir."

Lambert said nothing. He knew what was coming. He also knew he had to refuse it even though he wanted to agree with the R.S.M.

". . . so I was wondering, sir, if you could excuse them from roll call tonight."

"You know how I feel about it, sargnmajor. But the only thing we have left to hold us together is discipline. If we don't keep the men up to the mark, they'll fall apart. Then there will be burials every day."

"Of course, sir."

"Righto. That's settled."

The R.S.M. saluted.

Lambert saluted in return.

The men were dismissed. They limped off to their huts.

4

Dawson and Sykes watched them go. Sykes looking towards the limping men murmured, "Limpy's a real bastard. He should do something about their working conditions."

"What can he do. Hell, man, those Japs ain't going to listen to old Limpy."

"Maybe. But why worry. I'm knocking off. There'll be no bloody food left for me otherwise."

Dawson laid down his rag and began to scratch at his teeth with a grubby fingernail. "You know, Sykes, I think I'll take up this racket after the war."

"Which racket?"

Dawson indicated the latrines. "This. Attendant at a Gents."

"Gaw on." Sykes was interested but also cautious. "What's the future in it?"

Dawson shrugged. "I'm not sure. But I suppose you could be promoted to an inspector . . . or maybe be promoted to a bigger and better one."

"Yeah. Start in the provinces or the suburbs and eventually become mate-de-hotel of a bigger one. In the City or the West End."

"Mate-de-hotel?"

"French for manager."

"Oh. It sounds bloody posh for a lavatory. Still, there could be a few sidelines if you got a big place in the West End. You could flog contraceptives and telephone numbers." Dawson was an ambitious man in his own limitations.

"Sod that! I'm going to need all those telephone numbers for myself after the war. Boy are those sheilas going to go through hell when I get back. And talking of sheilas, what the hell is that——"

"I can't see anything," said Dawson.

"Well I bloody well saw her. A white sheila, but dressed in a kimono."

"You're nuts."

"I'll belt you one in a minute if you call me nuts again——"

"You're nuts . . . Christ!"

Dawson had also seen the girl.

So had half the camp. Mad Ike saw her as he moved about the compound looking for discarded cigarette butts. Big Peter, who went around the huts moaning, "My God, where are *those* Allies, where in God's name have they got to" saw her and moaned even louder. Clewes was pausing in his hunt for bed-bugs when he saw her.

She was tall, pale, fair, with hair that had almost been burnished white by the sun.

She stood on the step for a moment, between the two sentries who ignored her, and then, seeing that she had been seen and was being ogled, she disappeared back through the door.

Dawson and Sykes looked at each other for a full minute.

"Well . . . well . . . Yamamitsu . . . who would ever have thought old Yam-Yam had such good taste," said Dawson.

"Better tell Lambert."

"Why? She'd be no good for him. Or rather he'd be no good for her."

"You know the instructions. Everything any prisoner sees must be reported to the senior officer."

"You report it. I'll watch. I want to see this sheila again. I wonder where old Yam-Yam got her from? I'd give five years of my life to know," murmured Dawson.

5

Lambert was making his nightly tour of the huts. He was frowning. Two men were missing from the last hut. He entered the next. The hut leader, a prune-faced man named Thornton, saluted, and said there were three missing.

"Three? Missing? What the devil do you mean, 'missing'? What have they done? Vanished?" Lambert hated himself for saying that. But it had to be said, by him, by nobody else.

"The Japs, sir. They drove off with a party of five."

"When?"

"Before sundown, sir?"

"Did you see them go?"

"No, sir."

"Who did?"

"I—I don't know, sir."

Thornton was unhappy. But Lambert had no time for his feelings. The Japanese had taken five men. He felt a sudden cold stab of fear.

Five men.

With relatives, friends, hopes, sorrows, fears. One minute they had been there, had been part of the camp, of the camaraderie that had been slowly built up over the past three years. They had lived and suffered with the others. Suddenly, the guards had swooped. And the five had been whisked away.

"Find out who saw them go. And be quick about it."

"Then——?"

"Then be damned. I'll decide what then."

"Yes, sir!"

"Who were the five?"

Thornton gave Lambert their names.

"Any of them married?"

"Two, sir."

"Poor bastards," Lambert murmured, "five poor bastards."

"I agree, sir. Probably the Japs wanted a bit of entertainment after getting intoxicated on saki. It's happened before, sir. . . ."

Lambert wasn't listening. He was thinking of other men who had vanished. Occasionally, working parties had stumbled on what was left of them . . . swinging from trees with entrails hanging out like multi-coloured telephone wires.

Thornton said slowly. "They might have gone to the wharf."

"They might not, as well."

"Of course, sir."

Lambert walked out of the hut and into another. Some of the men watched his entrance with undisguised hostility. They disliked Lambert for trying to run the camp on military lines. He stopped before a man with a particularly ragged bandage.

"I thought I ordered you to have that changed."

"There aren't any clean ones, sir."

"There are! We had some washed ones back this morning. Get one in the morning."

Lambert moved on. He ordered one man to shave, another to get a haircut, rasping, "Where do you think you are, Chelsea?" Then he stomped out.

For a moment the hut was silent. Then a torrent of abuse broke out—all directed at Lambert. If he heard he showed no sign as he stomped across the compound. He was troubled. He had just heard about Sheppey.

6

Sheppey recovered consciousness with the bitter taste of something resembling decaying wood and sour fungus in his mouth. He shivered slightly as he dragged his way back to his bunk. Stabs of pain darted through his body. In a few seconds he was jerking spasmodically. He tested his physical condition by trying to stand up but it was too much of an effort, and he buckled back on to the bed. He heard his voice gabbling and mumbling, but he could do nothing to check it. It stuttered on until he became too hoarse to speak. It was some time before his mind regained its balance and he realised that he had been over the dividing line between sanity and madness. He swallowed hard and thought of cruder and more practical things.

But it was only a temporary respite. That rabbit punch of Sakamura's had damaged some of the delicate nerves linking Sheppey's spinal cord to his brain. His mind began to cloud over again. His reeling brain urged him to reach out for food that seemed to lie just out of reach. There were plates of steaming sausages and mash, a bottle full of raw, revitalising whisky: his nostrils twitched under the fragrant aroma of steak and onions. All he had to do was reach out for it. He imagined that the sweat and tears trickling down his face was alcohol.

He fought valiantly against these delusions. He knew that if he gave up there would be no hope of saving his sanity. He was in the middle of these struggles when Lambert found him.

"Shep——," Lambert was the only man who called the little science master that—"Shep, I hear you've had a rough time...."

Lambert couldn't see the little man in the gloom of the hut, couldn't see that his face was the face of a man in the throes of some horrible mental agony. Sheppey's eyes were bleak pebbles of pain as he tried to mumble a reply.

"Shep . . . tell me about it, Shep, all of it."

"Sa . . . Sakam . . . ura. Chopp . . . ed me . . . back of the neck. Nerves gone," gasped Sheppey.

"I'll get a doctor to have a look at you," said Lambert, moving swiftly from the hut.

He moved so swiftly that he did not see Sakamura with the posse of soldiers hiding beside the hut. Sakamura watched Lambert hobble swiftly away then he nodded to the soldiers. They moved towards the door of the hut.

It was completely dark inside the hut when Sheppey heard the heavy tramping on the bare boards. It stopped beside his bed. The soldiers bunched round it. They looked tough, menacing and wary. One of them motioned him forward. When Sheppey found it difficult to move they roughly grabbed him and half-carried and half-dragged him out of the hut. In that fashion they headed for the Administration Block.

Behind them walked Captain Sakamura.

He was grinning in anticipation. And he felt positively happy at what Lambert's reaction would be when he returned to find Sheppey had gone.

Chapter Eight

I

SHEPPEY was taken to a small room and booted through the door by his escort. Two hours passed before they returned for him. By then Sheppey had partly recovered.

In silence he and his escort ascended a flight of bare wooden stairs and finally halted before a solid-looking door. One of the soldiers knocked and entered. He returned in a few moments and ordered Sheppey to enter.

The first thing he noticed when he got in the room was the glass-framed portrait of the Emperor on the wall facing the door. It was the same as hundreds of others he had seen in newspapers and magazines—the rabbit-like face wore that unctuous smile that the Emperor always wore in public. His tired eyes took in the desk, papers and old-fashioned oil lamp; the two wooden chairs each side of the desk, the thickly carpeted floor. That carpet, Sheppey thought, seemed out of character with the room. But he had little time to think about it. For the man behind the desk had looked up from his papers.

It was Sakamura.

A Sakamura Sheppey had never seen before. The Captain was dressed in a splendid ceremonial uniform, laced with braid and insignias. He motioned the escort to leave the room, acknowledging their salutes with a wave of the hand. Then he looked at Sheppey; a long and careful stare.

Sheppey's heart started to thump.

"Do you know why you are here, little Sheppey?" Sakamura's voice was low and smooth.

Sheppey could only shake his head in reply.

"Ahhhh! You soon will. Sheppey, you see I have proof that you are behind the trouble on this island. I have some questions to ask you."

Sakamura's voice had lost its pleasantness, and now was hard and impersonal. Sheppey's breath caught in his throat. That underscored word "proof" had a chilling and dangerous ring about it.

"Proof, Captain?"

Sakamura nodded, and said, "But first let me know more about you. . . ."

So the interrogation began. Sakamura had Sheppey repeat every detail of his life until he had been brought to the camp. When Sheppey had finished he made him repeat it all over again. Finally he made Sheppey write it all down.

He read it for a moment, then with calculated deliberation he tore the sheets of foolscap he had provided the science master with into small squares. "That," he said, "is what I care for you. You are not worth more than the paper you have written on."

Sheppey said nothing. Things didn't seem to be shaping up too well.

"Confess . . . are you not behind the trouble?"

"No, Captain."

"You lie!"

"No, Captain."

Sakamura rose swiftly to his feet and smacked Sheppey across the face. "You are a liar. Say that."

"I—am—a—liar."

Looking closer at Sakamura, Sheppey saw that it had a certain glow about it. Then the Jap spoke again, "Well, well, little Sheppey, you admit that you are a liar. For that you must be rewarded."

With that Sakamura picked up a small stool that was hidden behind his desk and hurled it at Sheppey. He was taken by surprise and the stool cracked with painful force against his chest and stomach.

"Now confess more. Tell me about other plans you have helped to make."

Sheppey said there was nothing to say.

Sakamura slowly walked round from behind his desk and bent down to pick up the stool. He held it in one hand for a moment then flung it even harder than before at Sheppey. This time it caught him in the buttocks.

"Confess. . . ."

The confession business seemed to have become a mania with Sakamura. His questions came faster now and in shorter phrases. Hadn't Sheppey broken the camp wireless? Hadn't he helped Keiller to escape? Wasn't Lambert plotting some devilment? And so on, over and over again, clogging his mind, making it difficult to think.

"You are lying. . . !"

Sakamura's face suddenly exploded in a fit of passion. His lips twisted and curled back, showing his yellow teeth and bacteria-infected gums. With a squeal of fury he rushed from behind his desk and yanked Sheppey off his stool on to the floor. His mask of sanity had slipped completely; he had become a frothing-at-the-mouth maniac, kicking at Sheppey. He felt a crushing pain as the captain's boots caught his chest and stomach. Everything began to float before his eyes. Soon he had ceased to feel the blows.

When he came to he was huddled over the stool with Sakamura standing over him. With a last vicious kick the Captain returned to his desk, trembling with fury.

Again the questions started. But Sheppey noticed that Sakamura didn't seem to be taking any notice of his replies. His pen was racing over sheets of foolscap at amazing speed. Soon the questions tapered off into uncomfortable silence.

At last Sakamura looked up. "So—you will not confess. Very well I have written out a confession for you! You will sign it. I will tell you what it says." The captain began to read from the paper. . . .

"I confess to several acts of sabotage, which are itemised below, against the Imperial Forces of Japan. I have agreed to sign this confession without any pressure. I agree that it is true that these people are also implicated with me in planning acts of sabotage against the Imperial Forces of Japan. . . ."

There followed a list of practically every senior officer and important civilian prisoner in the camp. The "confession" said that Sheppey had revealed that between them they had taken part in over one hundred acts of sabotage. Sheppey had never taken part in one act of sabotage. . . and he had never heard anything at all about the other acts.

Yet Sakamura expected him to sign it. He knew why. He knew that the captain would keep this document as a sort of life line; when the Allies arrived he would produce it and use it in an attempt to justify the Special Executions he had staged.

But his audacity made Sheppey gasp. In a dazed voice, he mumbled, "You must think I'm mad to sign that. . . ."

"Shut up!" Sakamura screamed.

"I—will—not—sign."

For a moment there was silence in the room. Then Sakamura spoke again. "Very well, little Sheppey. I will sign it for you.

And because I have to, your fate will be even more unpleasant. . . ."

With that he banged on the bell button on his desk bringing the escort into the room instantly. A few curt orders in Japanese and the guards grabbed Sheppey. He was hauled from the room, with Sakamura's shouts echoing in his ears. He heard the words clearly, "Sheppey, it was a great pity you did not cooperate. . . ."

The group walked down the stairs and down to a basement. They came to a halt before a heavy bamboo-grilled door. He was pitched into the dark cavern behind the door. He did not bother to look around. He was too tired. In minutes he took the only way out of this unholy jam, by falling asleep on the cold, dank floor.

He awoke two hours later to find that he was in a dungeon. He had never known of its existence before, and had no recollection of it being dug by any of the prisoners. It was an earth-walled hole that seemed to be for ever pressing down on him, threatening to crush his tormented body out of existence.

Sheppey found that the hardest to bear was the loneliness. At first his mind was full of anger at the savage treatment meted out to him. But as time crawled by his mind once more started to dwell on fantasy.

Soon the fantasy had changed to real terror in the darkness of his cell. Not even a trickle of light came through the bamboo slots; he was that far below ground. The darkness was stifling and he found it harder and harder to keep control of his mind. General weakness forced him down on to the floor again and into a fitful sleep. Hardly had he closed his eyes than a nightmare engulfed his mind. He was jerked back to consciousness a slobbering wreck of a man.

Suddenly there was a noise outside the door and a bulging eye glared through the grille. Bolts were drawn back from the door and Sakamura stepped into the room.

"I trust that you have had a good rest. But now it is up. Your trial for espionage starts in a few minutes."

2

Sakamura had been delighted with his plans. He had grown bored with Special Executions. They seemed to have a sameness about them. They had lost much of their fun. He felt sure that the victims had decided not to play up to his whims. So when he had decided to execute Sheppey he had decided it would be a full dress affair. It was going to be a sort of public carnival, a show piece to prove that Sakamura was top dog.

At a little before midnight he had ordered the guards to summon all the prisoners from their huts and to have them paraded in the compound.

The compound was starkly lit by searchlights. At one end of it a platform had been erected. On the platform was a table, covered with a flag of the Rising Sun and a chair. The prisoners were ordered into lines about thirty feet before the platform. Guards patrolled between the lines, shouting for silence, and enforcing their shouts with jabs from rifle butts.

Then Sakamura appeared. He strutted across the compound, a bottle of saki in his hand. Lambert watched him approach. Straightened his back and stepped forward to meet the Japanese captain.

"What is the meaning of this?" Lambert's voice was cold.

"Patience, Lambert, have patience. All will be clear in a few moments."

Lambert hated the oily purr in Sakamura's voice. It was a danger signal that he had long come to recognise. But he had to press for an explanation. It was what the men expected of him. He would never let them down.

"Where is Sheppey . . . and the other five men?"

Sakamura looked at him for a moment then took a swig from the saki bottle. He savoured the drink in his mouth, then squirted it over Lambert.

Then he turned on his heel and walked over to the Administration Block to where Sheppey was immured.

3

Sheppey stumbled across the compound until he became aware that the other prisoners were all watching him. He stopped for a moment. Braced his thin shoulders, thrust his jutting jaw a little further ahead and tried to march.

He failed.

His feet got entangled with each other and he collapsed on the ground. Two guards jerked him to his feet. Finally he came to a halt before the platform. He was in a sort of no-man's land. Yards behind him were the first row of prisoners; Lambert, Archer, Beattie, Watkins, and many others he had caught a glimpse of. In front of him was Captain Sakamura, seated behind the table. The cold spotlights gave his face a yellowish pallor.

So the trial began.

Sakamura was the prosecutor. He was also the President of the court. Sheppey had no defending counsel. When Lambert stepped forward to protest, a guard clouted him in the ribs with a thick stick. Sakamura told Sheppey he could put any questions he liked, but that he must not waste time.

"The bastard wants this to be a fast moving non-stop revue," a hard voice grated from the rear ranks of the watching prisoners.

"If another man talks, I will order him to step forward to be executed. If he doesn't, I will select two men as a lesson. I will personally execute them," Sakamura said calmly.

He turned to Sheppey and said that the charge was sabotage against the Japanese Army. Had he anything to say in his defence?

Sheppey took a step forward, rising his head as he did so. "Captain, I completely deny the charge. It is without foundation——"

"That is for me to decide!"

"You are wrong, Captain."

Again Sheppey was cut short with, "I decide that. I say you are guilty."

Slowly picking up a sheet of paper, Sakamura demanded: "You signed this—yes?"

"No! You know you signed it."

"Please—you will not waste time making stupid accusations! Have your say and be silent."

Sheppey said nothing. He could see by the way Sakamura was looking at him that it would be pointless to say anything. Besides the captain had started to look bored. He nodded as he rose to his feet.

"I find the charge proved. You have been given every chance to defend yourself."

Pausing to look at some notes on the table, he continued, raising his voice as he did so: "I see no grounds for leniency. You have caused much trouble. Saboteurs always cause much trouble. So you are sentenced to death by shooting."

It was all over.

Sheppey knew he should have been frightened. Fear had been his constant companion ever since he had come to Blood Island. But he had lost it in the past few minutes. Now that he knew that his life was forfeit he had a dim feeling of relief.

He was almost annoyed by the angry murmur from the watching prisoners. He half turned to them, made an attempt at a shrug and turned back. He couldn't understand what they were angry about.

4

It was a little after 2 a.m. when the prisoners were roused once again to parade in the compound. The platform had been removed and a stake driven into the ground. Before the stake, at a range of fifteen yards, stood a line of eight Japanese, with rifles held loosely in their hands. The prisoners were herded to one side of the line.

Sheppey appeared. He looked calm and almost happy. The execution yard was not what he had expected. He had looked for a solid brick wall, with the wall well chipped at about the height of a man's chest. The solitary stake was a disappointment to him.

His hands were lashed to a post. The firing squad stiffened. A snake-faced sergeant seemed to be in charge. He gave a shout and eight barrels were focused on Sheppey.

Sakamura, standing well to one side, beamed at the watching prisoners. But they could not take their eyes off those guns. They wanted to close their eyes, to turn their heads. But they were held rigid by the spectacle of a man on the verge of violent death.

As the rifles lined up on Sheppey a terrible desire to live overpowered everything. He was going to be killed. But, dear God, he wanted to live!

He heard Sakamura's guttural shout, then a split second after the sharp clicks of rifle triggers. It was all over. It didn't hurt any more . . . his body felt lighter already. His head was swimming. He was floating.

Slowly things cleared and he saw that the Japanese firing squad was staring at him, one or two of its members sneering mirthlessly. Their rifle barrels were still levelled at him. It did not make sense. Then he realised what had happened. It had been a trick; a glorified version of Russian roulette.

There had not been any bullets in the guns in the first place.

His body soaked in sweat, sagged against the post. He wanted to vomit.

Then the guns were trained on him again. And again the farce was played out . . . with Sheppey still living. Six times the firing squad received the order "Fire!" Six times they pulled their triggers. And each time there were no bullets in the guns.

If Sheppey's wits had strayed before, they had gone completely at the end of the sixth time. There was no disguising the madness in his croaks and gurgles.

Lambert watched him with a feeling of deep loathing for everything Japanese. But as the firing squad lined up for the seventh time, with dawn starting to streak the sky, he noticed, suddenly, small things that were different about them now. They looked alert, restless, expectant like hounds on a leash. Sakamura too had lost his nonchalant air. His voice seemed harsher as he began to bawl out the words of command.

The soldiers fell into line. Lambert could see the concentration in their eyes, in every line of their squat, powerful, rigid bodies. They raised their rifles carefully at the squirming, mumbling Sheppey.

Lambert felt his own body go rigid as Sakamura's last shout was obliterated by the crash of shots. Sheppey's body jerked like a puppet; his mumblings were cut short in a ghastly scream.

It was all Lambert could do to stop himself spewing. He could not take his eyes off the dead man. He watched the dull red patch grow on his chest, and the slow drip of his life blood on the ground.

For Sheppey, Sakamura's little game was over.

For ever.

And ever.

"Amen," muttered Lambert.

Chapter Nine

I

THE sun's rays knifed over the horizon directly on to the corpse.

Sakamura watched the rays for a moment. Then he walked over to the post, unbuckling his sword as he did so. For a moment he peered at the lifeless Sheppey, then, casually he lifted his sword.

The blade had reached the height of Sakamura's shoulder tabs before Lambert realised what was going to happen.

"Don't, Sakamura, don't!"

Sakamura stopped and looked at Lambert. There was a mocking smile on his lips. By then the sword was high above his head.

For a split second life stood still.

Then the blade swished downwards. There was sickening crunch and Sheppey's head rolled on to the ground. A fountain of blood jetted high into the air from his severed neck. Sakamura held his sword at arm's length and let some of the blood fall on it. He was smiling broadly as he did so. The insane smile of a psychopath.

A wild scream broke from the front line of the prisoners. Then Watkins stepped forward a pace or two. He took one wild look about him, crouching as he did so.

Two guards raised their sub-machine-guns. Sakamura spun round, sword at the ready.

Watkins saw none of this. He was like some jungle animal, crazed by the sight of blood.

"Come back, you bloody fool!" Lambert shouted. "You can't do——"

"I'm taking that bastard with me. I'll wring his bloody neck if it's the last thing I'll do." Then Watkins released the mental brakes that had held him in check. Like a human turbine, he tugged and screamed. For a moment he didn't seem to move. Then he ran, then leapt and finally flashed over the ground at incredible speed.

But speed that could not outpace lead fired from a sub-machine-gun.

Watkins had covered two hundred feet, an incredible distance, considering the obstacles, when he was cut down.

The first burst, fired from his left flank, spun him round and round. He slid, at an angle, across the ground.

He looked as if he was skating on earth.

Then the second burst hit him. It started just below his arm-pit and stitched a stream of bullets into his side, from shoulder to hip bone.

But still Watkins ploughed on.

His face was twisted into a meaningless bundle of flesh. But his hands, aching to stem the flow of blood from his body, stretched instead before him. Clawing, clutching hands that sought for a grip on Sakamura's throat.

Watkins was only yards from the Japanese captain.

Then the third burst hit him.

It was a long one. A burst that held something of a desperate note about it. It started on the ground before Watkins. A concentrated symphony of fire from the execution squad and a score of guards. The opening shots sent stutters of dust sailing gaily into the air in Watkins' path.

Then the bullets reached him.

First it was his feet. Both legs were cut off from the ankle bone downwards. Then his knee joints were shattered. In seconds his pelvic circle was splintering through his torn flesh. Next to go was his abdomen. Followed by his stomach, chest, neck and face.

Watkins had given up caring after the burst that bit into his testicles.

He jack-knifed forward. Then, he leapt upright, as if his body refused to lie down. In a crazy gyroscope of a turn he twisted round and round.

The bullets thudding into his body seemed to make him revolve faster and faster.

Then, with a terrible final crash, he hit the ground. Clouds of dust swirled about his body, hiding its twitching, its goriness.

Sakamura strolled towards the carnage. For a moment he looked down at the body. Then he shrugged his shoulders and turned to face the silent prisoners.

"Lambert, step forward." His voice was flat and unemotional.

Lambert stepped forward.

Sakamura looked him up and down and then started to speak:

"These two men"—he swept his arm in a vague semi-circle in the direction of Sheppey and Watkins—"are a lesson and a warning to all others who either defy or commit acts of sabotage against the authorities.

"Lambert, I am holding you responsible for the future conduct of your men. As you are responsible, I want you to understand that any future executions will take place only because you did not exercise proper control over these men. I warn you, Lambert, that things are going to be much tougher from now on. It is, as you say in England, time for the kid gloves to come off."

Sakamura made a motion of removing a pair of gloves before continuing:

"But it is not enough that only two men should be punished for the sins of you all. . . ."

He paused to let his words sink in. Then in a loud, theatrical voice he went on:

"You have asked where the other five men were, Lambert. You have asked me many times in the past few hours. . . ."

Once again Sakamura paused to let the cold chill of fear steal through Lambert's body.

". . . you will now have the answer. It is not what you expected. . . ."

Sakamura spun round on his heel. . . .

To Marty Nicholls it was a movement that curiously brought to him memories of the past. A past that seemed part of another world. A world long dead. A world that centred round the powerful arc lights of a television studio.

2

Marty Nicholls had been the first to make a successful consummation of his marriage with television. He had been in on the early beginning. The days when British television ran on a pinch-penny budget producing pinch-penny programmes.

Marty had made a success of almost everything he had turned to. Save one thing.

His life.

He had made money, lots of it, had bought almost all the things he could buy with money.

But his life had always been empty of the one thing he craved after above all else: happiness. Women became embarrassed when he looked at them. They squirmed a little and averted their faces from his gaze.

Marty *was* rather a repulsive man to look at. He had a shapeless and blubbery mountain of a body that sagged and flopped inside the folds of his wrinkled clothes. On a hot day he gave people the impression that he would melt into a boneless mass of gelatinous flesh. Whenever he looked in a mirror he hated himself. And he hated all those who looked at him with distaste.

Especially women.

Especially the prostitute who had turned him away the evening before he had flown out of London to Malaya to do initial research for a documentary he was writing and producing for television.

It had happened over three years ago. But every second of it all had been burnt deeply into Marty's mind. . . .

He had left the studios on a warm night in July. It had been a hard and exacting day for Marty. The sort of day which he relished. For on the studio floor or in the control box Marty was happy. There he was a professional, working among other professionals, who measured him only by his professionalism. What he looked like didn't matter; it was what he did, and how he did it, that counted.

As he had left the studio he had bumped into an attractive young woman on the pavement. He had never seen her before. But the sight of her clean-limbed young body brought on a familiar stirring inside his clothes. He felt a prickly feeling and he knew he would have to do something about it.

He walked after her, not with any intention of approaching her, but rather to feed his eyes on her firm, slender body.

She sensed that he was following her for she turned around. There was a blank look on her face that quickly turned to loathing. She quickened her pace, then crossed the road.

It only increased the yearning coursing through Marty's body.

He liked the feeling. It made him uneasy, but pleasantly uneasy. He felt sexually hungry under the pressure within his body.

His mind was made up. As he had made it up many many times before.

He would buy a woman. She would barter her body for the feel of some of the wad of notes bulging in his wallet.

But first he would have a drink.

By now the street lamps were lit. Most of the shop fronts in Regent Street were shuttered, but behind the bolted doors he could still hear signs of activity.

London fascinated him, with its theatres, its air of business, its pageants. Marty had been born in the country, near Newmarket. He had never quite thrown off the air of perplexity and curiosity that a countryman has for a big city. It made him an interested observer of even the most trivial things.

The bus drivers wore their thick serge coats and had even wrapped multi-coloured check scarves round their necks. Marty thought they must be mad to dress like this in the middle of summer, albeit an English summer.

He noticed that the policemen were red-faced as they stood at their points, arms flapping this way and then that.

The girls hurrying through the streets were wearing thin print dresses of the latest creation; they clung to them wetly, accentuating their breasts, buttocks and thighs. Most of the older women had sensibly stuck to the fashion of the previous year.

Middle class men hurried along the pavements with an air of definite purpose that seemed to go hand in glove with their spreading waistlines.

In Trafalgar Square the fountains spouted thick white plumes of spray that must have been very disconcerting to the flocks of pigeons congregating there. At vantage points, newsvendors were selling the last editions of the evening papers, their cries of "Starnewsstandardlatest" rising above the blare of traffic. But the barrow boys, snuggled in side streets, were having a thin time of it selling the rotting fruit and roasted nuts.

Marty spared them a quick glance and walked on. The doors of the public houses swung steadily to and fro on their well-oiled hinges as an unbroken stream of customers made their way to the bars, behind which glass and pewter and brass glittered.

Marty joined the throng leaning against one of the bars, ordered a brandy, downed it in one gulp, and repeated the performance several times.

By now his hunger had grown to a throbbing inside his clothes. The liquor had also made him feel sorry for himself.

He felt he was the loneliest man in the world. It made him weep a little inside. And it helped to sharpen his longing.

So he set out to do something about it.

He walked down narrow and shadowy side streets where second-hand furniture shops jostled against the grocers who probably took bets on the side and the strong-smelling fish shops.

Down there too lived the street women. At dusk, singly, in pairs, sometimes in groups, they walked slowly and purposefully to their posts. Many of them are running to fat. All of them have over-blackened eyelids and scarlet mouths which break into automatic smiles whenever a man looks their way.

They teetered along on high heels, swinging their capes of worn silver-fox expertly. If a man paused, one of them sidled up to him with a sensuous, "Like to come home for a while, darling. . . ?"

They waited at street corners, in shop doorways and café fronts. To while away the time between customers, they pulled steadily at cigarettes which glowed as scarlet as their mouths in the darkness.

A few passed themselves off as French, ending their invitations with "Cheri". They traded on the fact that anything French appealed to some men. But their soft Irish brogues made the French phrases sound ridiculous.

They watched Marty come and they moved closer together. They thought he was one of those "barmy blokes" who got a thrill out of fingering them in the street. They had decided he was a "pervit" after some had taken him back to their shabby rooms. They had black-listed him.

No amount of Marty's money could buy his way off that list. Only he didn't know that. He didn't have an inkling as he ambled towards a woman.

"You want to take me home? I'm booked!"

"Now. I won't take long."

There was a pause. Then the woman shrugged her shoulders and began to step back to her little piece of shadow, flanked on either side of the brilliantly lit window displays.

"I said I was booked. Got a date. Try some of the others."

"I want you. You name the price, I'll pay."

Her voice jeered at him, "Anything you'd pay wouldn't be enough. . . ."

"You don't know——"

"But some of the others do——"

The woman took a glance down the street. She could see two of the other girls at the corner, but there was no sign of any of the boys. She swore, using a filthy word.

"You coming, or not?"

"Beat it. I'm tired of being annoyed by you. I don't want you hanging around. You see we've found out what you *really* are."

"What I *really* am?" He was furious now. "That is quite something. You telling me what I am. What the hell do you think you are."

"I'm a whore," she said, simply. "But even a whore has a right to share what she's offering with who she likes. I don't want to share it with you. . . ."

She spun round on her heel. . . .

The way Sakamura had spun round.

3

Slowly Sakamura came to a stop.

Every prisoner stiffened.

Through the prison gates came a truck. It was travelling slowly. It came on and on towards Sakamura. Then, when it was a few yards from him it came to a stop. The captain turned back to look at Lambert. Then he said, "Here is the answer as to what happened to those five men. . . ."

Chapter Ten

I

SAKAMURA clapped his hands loudly.

The truck swung round, agonisingly slowly, until its tailboard was facing the line of prisoners. A cloth flap was tied down to the tailboard blocking any view of the inside of the truck. Sakamura clapped again. The flap was pulled aside. The prisoners saw that monkey face of a Japanese soldier. He climbed out and threw a ragged salute at Sakamura. Then he turned back to the truck.

"Out, out, quickly, quickly," he shouted.

Over the tailboard clambered the first of the missing five men. On his shoulder he had a sack. In minutes the five men were on the ground, standing by a small pile of sacks.

Sakamura walked towards the prisoners. "The sacks," he said, "hold all your mail. It has been held by the camp authorities in the hope that it might induce you all to behave yourselves. But it has had no effect. So, regrettably"—though his voice belied the words—"I shall have to refuse to hand it over."

He turned to the monkey-faced soldier. He went into the cab of the truck and reappeared with a drum of petrol. He walked over to the sacks and poured the fuel over them. Then he dropped a match on the sacks. They gushed into flame.

There was not a murmur from the prisoners.

Each man was an isolated island as he watched the flames curl and blacken the letters. Each man had his own vision of some loved one far away in England. A wife, a sister, a brother, a sweetheart, a mother, a father; crouched across a table or bent forward in an air raid shelter, scribbling words of love and encouragement: words that would have meant so much to these human islands on an inhuman island.

But nothing showed on their hard, impassive faces.

Sakamura couldn't understand the silence. He had heard that the British were so sentimental; he had heard that they would weep over the death of a pet dog or the sight of a beautiful sunset. He had heard that English soldiers, cut off, would make suicidal journeys through enemy-held positions to collect the mail. He had expected a mad rush to extinguish the flames in an attempt to save the mail.

But the prisoners did not even stir.

Sakamura shrugged. He ordered the men to return to their huts. This had been an anti-climax to the gory drama he had stage-managed in the past few hours.

Colonel Yamamitsu watched the men straggle back to their huts. He also shrugged and turned to go into his bungalow. Yamamitsu knew how he would spend the rest of the day. First he would gorge himself on prawns and saki. Then he would play his favourite recordings. Then he would feast himself on the white geisha girl.

Then high in the sky came an unfamiliar noise. The spluttering of an aeroplane engine.

2

Colonel Yamamitsu rushed to the edge of the balcony and peered into the dark blue sky.

He saw nothing.

Lambert was halfway to his hut when he heard the noise in the sky. He was deep in thought and relief; he had feared that the prisoners might have made an attempt to salvage the mail; he sensed that was what Sakamura had hoped for. It would have given the Captain the excuse to mow down a few score more men. He wondered how long it would be before Sakamura would completely do away with excuses. Then he heard the noise. He looked into the sky.

He saw nothing.

The men looked into the sky. They scanned it with red-rimmed tired eyes.

They saw nothing.

Lambert's heart started to beat faster. It pulsed against his ribs, making it painful to breathe. At first he thought it might be an air drop; that Keiller had got through after all. He had a wonderful vision of paratroopers dropping out of the sky into the compound and wiping out the guards.

He thought that until he recognised it was the throb-throb of a solitary engine he had heard. An engine of a small machine, incapable of carrying paratroopers.

He decided it was a fighter. And even as he had decided that, came a change in the constant tune of the engine. It took on a discordant note, became rough, unmusical.

Then it missed a beat.

And the hearts of all the prisoners missed a beat with it.

Lambert knew the pilot was in trouble . . . and he knew too that the pilot was an Allied one. He didn't know how he knew it. *He just knew it.*

3

For Captain Joe Bellamy, United States Air Force, it was his last patrol.

The war was over.

Just like that. One day he, and millions of others had been fighting "them"—the nebulous name for the enemy. Then had come Hiroshima. And as quickly as that—or as quickly as it had taken an atom bomb to drop from the belly of a giant bomber on to the Japanese city—the war had been over. Two missions had brought an end to six years of bitter and bloody fighting.

Two missions, Bellamy mused. Two goddamned missions. Hell, he had flown fifty times that number, and he had never been able to bring the war to an end. Bellamy was a complex man; his brain never stopped turning and puzzling behind his dark, rugged face.

Bellamy had greeted the end of the war with mixed feelings. He was glad it was over, because it meant that men would no longer die.

But he would miss it.

He would miss the chance to adding more little rising sun insignias to the ten already painted on his engine cowling. Each sun was a silent testimony to the fact that ten Japanese bombers and Zero fighters had gone down in flames beneath his stuttering guns. Bellamy had enjoyed every moment of those killings.

He had gone some of the way to settling scores with the Japanese. He had gone some of the way to avenging his father who had died on a stricken cruiser in the metal massacre of Pearl Harbour.

He had avenged his father on his first mission almost two years ago, when he had found the Japanese on that beach; he couldn't remember what beach; they all seemed the same to him. But he could never forget those Japs . . . and his first kill.

He would always remember the all-embracing thrill, a combination of sensuality and fear, he had felt as his plane had screamed towards the Japs in a power dive. He remembered the savage yammering of his multiple machine-guns, spitting death at the Japs before they realised it. He would always remember the sand kicking up in a hundred tulips and the Japs scythed down as his shells scissored through them. It had been a good feeling. A feeling that he had done something worthwhile. Something important.

He would remember that time as long as he lived. And the time after, when he had shot down his first Jap. It had been a bomber. A cumbersome thing against his silver-bellied salmon of the sky.

Bellamy had sat on its tail for mile after sky mile. After his first burst the side of the bomber had been zipped open and one of the crew had gone twirling to his death in the shark-infested sea below.

He had remembered his tightened grin about it. Japs, he had thought, were only good for shark meat.

And this was his last patrol. A patrol he did not have to make. Lefty and Chuck had asked him to do it. He remembered how the two had come to him. Fresh-faced, despite the fact that they had both completed one arduous operational tour, giving the Japanese hell with their cannons and rockets.

"Say, skip," Chuck had said, "we've just taken over a Jap flop house, complete with women."

"Yea, and we want to stake our claim before the rush starts," Lefty had added.

"And knowing you ain't interested in broads, we thought you might oblige us by doing this last damned patrol. . . ."

Bellamy had taken the patrol. A pointless patrol. But the High Command had said it had to be made. They felt there might be the chance that some of the Japs had not heard the war was over.

So he had taken off. As he had prepared himself for the flight he could hear the sounds of revelry coming from the flop house across the road from his hut. As he had climbed through clouds above the jungle, he mulled over Chuck's remark that he wasn't "interested in broads." He found the remark funny. Yet his smile was grim and rather bitter as he thought about it.

His mind went back to his wedding. Shortly after it had come his posting to a combat squadron. He remembered that day; one of thrill and black despair. At the end of it he had hurried home to Desmonde with the news. It was a surprise visit. He had managed to get a short furlough at the last moment. To celebrate it he had brought a bottle of hard-to-get real whisky (the label said it had been brewed in the Scottish Highlands), a cold, cooked chicken and a box of special chocolates.

He had been excited; it was going to be his last night with Desmonde for a long, long time.

He had opened his door with his key and had tiptoed into his flat. Music had reached him from the bedroom; soft and inviting music. He had tiptoed across to the door, smiling as he did so, and gently opened it.

Then his world had crumbled. Time seemed to have stood still. And Desmonde and the man, taken completely by surprise, had not moved. The shock of finding his wife in bed with another man had twisted a deep wound in Bellamy's soul. . . .

He swung his Thunderbolt down through the cloud. Chuck was right. He wasn't interested in women. Not after what he had seen in that bedroom. He had divorced Desmonde shortly after that. But it had not healed the wound. Nothing would, he said, as he sent the fighter howling towards the tree tops.

Then the engine had missed a beat. From beneath the cowling came spasmodic coughings. Then he saw black oil gush from the engine, smearing the perspex on the cockpit.

The plane started to plunge like a coffin towards the ground. He jacked back the hood and freed himself from the seat straps. The wind whipped at him as he swung over the side. He would have to be quick. Very, very quick.

For a second he rested on the wing. Then he had slipped into space. He wondered if he should pull the ripcord.

Nobody would miss him.

He would miss nobody.

He looked down. The ground was hurtling towards him.

He opened his parachute with a mechanical tug on the ring.

4

Kate Keiller stood in the doorway of the hospital hut and looked across the compound. She could feel the cooling breeze fanning her face, nudging through the breaks in her flimsy cotton dress.

If she looked to the left she could see the mountain peaks as faint shadows against the hazy skyline. Somewhere beyond the mountains, Father Anjou had said, a British army was thrusting onwards to rescue them.

She prayed they would come soon.

Her mind went to her husband. He was out there somewhere, in the steamy, swamp-infested jungle . . . hurrying to meet the soldiers. She prayed even harder.

Then she turned and went into the hut to pacify a whimpering woman in a far bed.

She did not see the young Japanese soldier, who was watching her from the corner of the next hut. He moved away, towards the kitchen. Tonight was to be his night. The night he would have Kate Keiller. But he needed help; it would have to be planned carefully.

He knew who the weaklings among the women prisoners were. He knew it by listening to the gossip of his fellow guards. He had a good idea who he could bribe, bully or coerce to help him get the white woman where he wanted her.

He entered the cookhouse.

Two women worked there. They were old, Chinese, but well fed. It was a privileged position. In the kitchen one had first pick at the food. And not only first pick, but as much as one wanted.

The two women, brewing gruel, swung to face the soldier. They cowed back when they saw the stick in his hand. He pointed it at the older of the two women.

"You—go now," he snapped.

"But——"

"Go," he screeched.

She moved in a half skip across the room. She bowed as she passed him. The youth was impatient. He swung the stick, striking her across the shoulders. She whimpered and fled from the kitchen.

The Jap closed the door.

There was a heavy stillness about the hut. The only sound was the bubbling gruel on the wood-fuelled stove.

He moved to the centre of the room. He took his time, savouring his power. He had never had anybody frightened or cowed before him until now. Where he had come from, a small village a hundred miles outside Tokyo, he had not frightened anybody, save an occasional cat or dog. But that did not count.

The villagers, even his own family, had treated him as something akin to the village idiot of rural England. Not to be taken seriously. The girls had laughed at him too. Seeing this had made his father unhappy. He knew it would cost him much to find his son a bride. And when the youth had wanted a woman he had had to hire one from the House of Women in the market place.

But now. . . .

Now he was somebody.

He said to the woman, backed up against the wall and grinning at him, "You want to make me pleased—yes?"

She nodded vigorously and smirked.

"Good. You do something for me?"

"Yes . . . anything." She tugged at her skirt, trying to look provocative. but only succeeding to look pathetic.

The youth leered. "Not you. You no good for Japanese lord. But you take message to Missee Kate Keiller. Now! Move," he shouted, raising his stick.

"But. . . ."

She didn't want to go. She was fond of Kate Keiller; Kate was a woman who worked tirelessly for the welfare of the prisoners.

"Why you not have me? I much more experienced than white woman. I know many, many things which I pleased to show Japanese lord. . . ."

She was used to being raped. But it would be terrible for Kate Keiller.

The youth moved forward. "You not waste time. You fetch Kate Keiller. . . ."

"—I no know where she is," the old woman tried to smile enticingly.

"Missee Keiller in hospital hut. I see her. You go fetch. Not say I want to see her. You say other woman faint in kitchen or something like that."

The old woman made one last desperate try to stall him. "She no good for you . . . today . . . any day. Me different."

The youth lost his patience and lashed out with his stick. He swung the woman round, throwing her across the rough wooden kitchen table as he did so. Then his stick rose and fell with monotonous regularity, slashing across her back and buttocks. She screamed as it did so.

Finally she broke away and ran for a corner. From there she spoke.

"I—I fetchee Kate Keiller now."

The youth stood back.

"You fetch quickly. But you die very slow death if you say I here."

"I no want to die. I fetch quickly. . . ."

5

Dusk was falling over the women's camp. And as it approached Kate Keiller wondered where Mrs. Beattie was. Mrs. Beattie was her chaperone, ever since the incident after the funeral. Then she saw a figure approaching in the gathering gloom. She knew it wasn't Mrs. Beattie because the figure was too bent and old.

Then she recognised the woman who worked in the kitchen.

"Missee Keiller . . . ?"

"Yes?"

"You come quickly kitchen please. Other woman badly burnt."

"I . . . one moment. I will get some bandages."

Kate Keiller hurried to a wall cupboard and took the equipment she would need, including a long pair of surgical scissors. She hurried back to the door.

"You had better stay here. Mrs. Beattie should come shortly. Tell her where I am."

The woman cringed back and said, rather too eagerly, "I tell her. You hurry. . . ."

Kate Keiller hurried towards the kitchen, clutching the scissors in her hand.

The youth saw her come. Saw that she was moving quickly, but without fear. He stood behind the door, pulling it ajar. Just before she reached the hut the curfew bell rang. He smiled. Things had turned out better than he had even planned. The approaching woman could not go out after the curfew bell unless she was escorted by a Japanese soldier. So if she tried to run away he could shoot her. But she would know that. So, he mused, she would not run. The hut was set apart from the others, so nobody would hear her screams.

And he would make her scream all right. . . .

He moved to the table and snuffed out the candle. Now the only light came from the stove.

Kate Keiller burst into the hut. Then she stopped. The lack of light warned her something was wrong. She took a step backwards. As she did so the door slammed shut behind her. Even as she turned a hand gripped her shoulder. She pulled away, and there came the sound of her dress tearing.

"You . . . !"

"Yessss. Meeee."

She stood there for a moment, terrified, linked to the youth by the piece of frayed material.

"You be nice me," he smirked, "you get plenty rewards. Many bars of chocolates and soap."

"No!"

Her scream filled the hut.

The youth tightened his grip, getting more purchase on the dress. Then he snatched downwards, tearing it off her shoulder.

She crossed her hands protectively across her bared bosom, stepping back as she did so.

The youth was smiling. His tunic was undone. He was thinking that if the villagers saw him now they would revise their opinion of his prowess.

He followed her across the room, or rather stalked her, until she was cornered. He raised the stick, "You be quiet. I be very kind to you. You maybe even come home to Japan with me. . . ."

That, he thought, would make his village sit up. . . .

"No . . . no," she whispered.

The youth dropped his stick and lunged at her. She saw the sweat glistening on his narrow chest in the light from the fire.

She knew what she had to do. She knew she had little time to do it in.

She would have to kill him.

The thought terrified her. To kill a man, even a man about to rape her, sent shudders of fear through her mind.

But she had to do it.

For herself.

For her husband, out in the jungle.

He pressed harder on her shoulder, forcing her down on to her knees. His touch made her flesh burn. His sour breath fanned her face.

She had to do it.

Quickly. Without thinking.

But she had to do it.

She did.

As his hand groped for her she struck. She struck, without thinking, quickly—*as she knew she must*—with the scissors. They made a puncturing sound as they pierced the youth's stomach. Then it was like a razor going through butter.

The youth's gasp died on his lips. His last thoughts, as he collapsed on Kate Keiller, were of his village and the villagers.

He knew agonising defeat in his dying moments.

He would certainly be called an idiot now . . . to be killed by a weak white woman as he was about to rape her.

That was the greatest insult he had ever suffered.

Chapter Eleven

I

FOR long minutes Kate Keiller lay there with the youth pressing down on her. Then she became aware of something warm and sticky dripping against her arm. Blood! Twisting, she became aware of the youth's eyes. They were a light glossy brown. The whites were yellow. And the sight of them snapped something in her mind. Pushing the youth away with all the force she could muster, she dashed across the kitchen, flung open the door, and began to scream.

Her hysterical screams broke the brooding silence of the camp. They were answered at first by a hubbub of noise as women prisoners crowded the doorways of their hovels. Then a searchlight was flipped on at the main gate. It caught Kate Keiller and held her there, as a guard took aim, centring his machine-gun on her frail, lonely and half-naked figure.

Captain Sakala was busy opening a fresh packet of chocolate bars in his hut when he heard the screaming. He cursed to himself and walked to the door.

Sergeant Nagaliki ran towards the kitchen. Behind him came three soldiers. The four closed in on Kate Keiller, weeping brokenly between her shrieks. They snatched at her arms and Nagaliki slapped her hard several times across the face to quieten her.

His English wasn't very good. What he had grasped had come from American paper-back novels. He said repeatedly, "You shut up now, sister. You shut up now or I shut you up for good, pronto."

From the huts an angry murmur had started to drift into the night air. Guessing much what had happened, and assuming that at least one of the soldiers now surrounding Kate Keiller was the rapist, catcalls, jeers and oaths came louder and louder from the women.

It only made Captain Sakala, approaching the kitchen hut, look more ridiculous. He tried to combat it by stiffening his back and twisting his face into a deep frown. Reaching the kitchen hut, he lifted his arms and faced the huts from where the abuse was coming.

"Silence. No more noise." His voice sounded strangely ineffectual.

It had no effect. Kate Keiller was loved and respected by almost all the women.

Sakala's voice rose to a high-pitched banshee wail. It had no effect. He looked ridiculous. The women thought he looked ridiculous. So did the guards. What was worse, Sakala knew he looked ridiculous.

He hated that. Hated the way the women stared at him. Japanese women didn't look at him in the way the white women did. Japanese women looked at him with respect and modesty.

So, he thought, did Mala. But she was different. She was half-oriental anyway, and could appreciate the special type of beauty of the male Japanese. And Sakala thought he was above the average in that special kind of beauty.

But the jeering women made him angry. A more intelligent man would have ignored their abuse and taken Kate Keiller off to the Administration Block. The other prisoners would not have dared to follow.

Sakala, sweating, with the bars of chocolate in his tunic melting, snapped an order to the guards.

Two stepped away from Kate Keiller, raising their Tommy-guns as they did so.

Another ran to the gate, shouting orders to the gate towers. The searchlight swung away from Kate Keiller towards the huts.

But the noise showed no signs of abating. By now too the women were spilling from the huts into the compound, hissing, jeering, waving their bony fists as they did so.

Sakala could feel the sweat dripping off his nose—and the chocolate seeping through his belt to his stomach.

He was scared.

Being scared, he panicked.

He barked an order.

The two Tommy-gunners, their hard faces masked in sweat and grime, went down on their knees. They levelled their guns and opened fire. Their bullets stitched a pattern in the dust around the women at several huts. Several of the women crumbled to the ground.

The machine-gunner on the gate, always looking for an

opportunity to shoot at something to relieve the monotony, also panicked and opened fire. But his aim was too high. He shot down a line of washing just beyond the huts.

The shooting went on for several minutes; the tommy-gunners firing short bursts as they swung their guns in a forty-five degree arc.

Then they stopped.

The silence could be heard. It was that loud.

Nagaliki relaxed his hold slightly on Kate Keiller's arm. She, her lips pressed back from her teeth, relaxed slightly and looked up.

Nagaliki and Sakala spoke simultaneously.

Nagaliki said, "There's blood on this woman's arm . . ." and for a moment he thought she had been injured by the firing from the machine-gunner at the gate.

"She lives . . . that is all right." Sakala wasn't interested in Nagaliki's gabbling. He had seen the bodies strewn around the doorways of the huts, and he wondered what he would tell Yamamitsu.

He began to bark orders. Guards, who had hurried up, began to go round the huts, bayonets and rifles at the ready. From the huts came the sounds of quiet whimpering and moaning. Sakala heard it and became angry.

Turning to Kate Keiller, who he felt was somehow responsible for all the trouble, he snarled, "Well . . . ?"

She said nothing.

He slapped her.

A guard said, "She came from the kitchen."

"And there is blood on her arm, but there is no cut to explain it," added Nagaliki.

"Search the kitchen," ordered Sakala.

Two guards moved towards the hut.

Sakala turned on Kate Keiller. "Why do you scream?"

"I—I. . . ." But Kate Keiller, her mind in a whirl, could think of nothing to say.

Sakala asked the question again, louder and firmer.

Then a soldier came hurrying from the hut, nearly tripping himself up in the swift flow of words that tumbled from his lips. He had a lisp, which didn't make it any easier. But Sakala grasped the gist of it. He swung back to Kate Keiller.

"You kill Japanese soldier!" Then he struck her, very fast

and very hard, with his balled fist. He struck her again. And then again. Her head swung one way and then another.

In the huts, looking from the doors and the mat-covered windows, the women winced as they watched Sakala administering the beating. They searched their minds for some way to revenge Kate.

One by one their eyes fastened on Mala, Sakala's whore.

She was stretched out on her bunk. She had heard the gunfire, but she had paid no attention to it. She was a simple girl; she could never understand gunfire and war. She could only understand one thing. Love. Her mother had taught her how to love. She ate, thought and dreamed of love. She did not intrigue and she said nothing malicious about anybody.

She could not understand what the looks she got from the other women meant. She could not place the tension that seemed to be directed at her.

Sakala had killed several women. Now he was beating Kate Keiller. And for that his woman was going to suffer.

But Mala had no idea.

2

Yamamitsu choked on a prawn when Sakamura hurried in and told him there had been an incident at the women's camp. He gulped when he heard that several of the women had been shot.

"Which women? Young ones? That Sakala, I always said he was a fool. . . ."

"And, if you remember, I didn't disagree with you," Sakamura said smoothly.

It had been in the balance as to who would take command of the women's camp: Sakala or Sakamura, Sakala had won because he was stupid. Yamamitsu said it only needed a stupid man to look after the women.

Yamamitsu said nothing for a few moments. He was remembering the faces and figures of several young girls his eyes had cast over in the past. He had marked them down for future use. What a waste it would be if Sakala had shot them. There was only one way to find out. Scoffing a prawn he snapped to Sakamura: "You had better get up there at once. Before he kills them all. If necessary, send him back here to report to me. Let me know as soon as you have some facts."

"I cannot order him back to report to you," said Sakamura smoothly, "We are of the same rank." He knew that Yamamitsu had been holding up his promotion for over a year.

"From this moment you are acting major. I will arrange for it to be put in writing."

"Shall I get Imperial Headquarters to confirm it?"

"Yes . . . yes. Get on with it."

Sakamura saluted and walked out.

While he ordered a car and four guards to be ready for him, the fat interpreter typed out a draft which confirmed his promotion. Sakamura returned to collect it, read it for a moment, re-read it, smiled in satisfaction and pocketed it. Then his car left the camp at high speed.

He was happy. He had been promoted. He had a good chance of taking over the women's camp. But he was slightly worried too. He hoped nothing had happened to Kate Keiller.

Sakamura's eyes had often stared at the dark-haired, smooth-skinned woman in the past months.

3

They had heard the firing in the men's camp. Some had said it was the advancing Allies fighting through to release them.

Dawson and Sykes sat on their bunks at the end of their hut and mulled it over. Between their bunks was the hut bucket, which was used after curfew.

They listened to the running commentary of the men looking through the windows.

"Christ, the whole sky's lit up. . . ."

"Yea . . . they're dropping flares. . . ."

"Bloody fool. That's the moon coming up. . . ."

"Flares, I tell you. I even saw the planes lit up in them. . . ."

"Lot of crap," said Sykes. "A lot of eyewash. I reckon it's a party up at the women's camp."

Nobody paid any attention to this remarkably accurate forecast. Everybody was too bent on looking for the impossible; the sight or sound of relieving forces.

"Still, they say there's a lot of activity going on at Yam-Yam's bungalow," cut in Dawson.

"Probably only Limpy Lambert protesting about the noise before he knows what it's all about."

4

In the senior officer's hut Lambert had also heard the firing. Several of the other officers came to his partitioned-off room. They stood around Lambert in the half darkness and discussed what it all meant.

"It might well be that one of our advance patrols has clashed with a Jap patrol."

But, quietly and firmly, Lambert told them not to let wishful thinking interfere with cold logic. For a start, Lambert reasoned, the firing seemed to be coming from the wrong direction for it to suggest a clash between the Allies and the Japanese.

"Gentlemen, at a rough guess, I would say that it was coming from the women's camp."

There was silence.

"I know how you all feel. But keep it to yourself. Above all, don't discuss such a possibility with Beattie. He has a wife and child there, in case any of you have forgotten."

An officer, who had been looking from the windows came back and reported.

"The Japs seem quite excited. The sentries are jabbering like monkeys down at the gate——"

"That's all they are, bloody chimps," said a beefy R.A.F. officer.

"Stow it," somebody called out.

The officer went on with his report. "The gate guards are all excited. Yamamitsu has sent his two sentries off with Sakamura. Everybody seems to be running round in circles."

There was silence.

Then somebody said: "Let's grab the camp."

Another silence.

It was broken by Lambert saying, "Too risky. But we can use this to our own advantage. I want to find out who the woman is at Yamamitsu's house. I want to see how far the Japs have got in repairing the radio." He looked at the Dutchman Van Elst. "And if we can use this opportunity to break into the Japs' ammunition hut and sabotage or steal supplies, then let's do it."

Nobody said anything.

Lambert peered at them in the gloom and went on, "It's too risky stealing guns. You know the way they are racked around the wall—they would be missed. But they can be damaged. And some water in the cartridge boxes and then the lids put back should take the sting out of the ammunition."

"Where would we get the water from?" somebody asked.

Lambert smiled one of his too rare smiles and said, "Use your imagination, David."

David used his imagination and gave a dry chuckle.

"We know the lay out of the ammo hut. We also have a copy of the key. Even though it is made of wood it should do the trick. But I don't want any guns taken. For a very obvious reason. They would be missed. And we would have no place to hide them. But, on the other hand, we could always find a place to stack away a dozen or two grenades."

There were murmurs of agreement.

"The boxes of grenades are placed in the left hand corner of the ammo hut," Lambert went on. "There are eight cases of fifty. What I suggest to the two officers picked for this assignment is this. . . . ."

The officers listened in silence.

When he had finished somebody asked, "Why don't we just blow the ammo hut up, colonel?"

"I'm sure we would be successful if we tried it. But it could force Yamamitsu into doing the very thing I am trying to avoid—a massacre of the prisoners in reprisal. The Japs are jittery enough. There is no news coming through. They are worried. A lot more worried than we probably realise. They can't make it out. They know that something big has happened. They know that we have a pretty good idea what that something is. Remember too that they must have guessed that we only knocked their radio out so that it would delay them knowing whatever we know. And also they have not had any visitors from the mainland, neither have supplies come through.

"Yamamitsu must be having sleepless nights. I think he is on the verge of doing something desperate. If we blew the ammunition up, he would probably crack up completely. He'd probably use what ammunition that was not in the hut to have a blood bath with the prisoners in both camps. Then the Japs would make a run for it."

David said, "What puzzles me, sir, is why nobody has arrived to tell him the war is over."

"It's clear enough to me, David. The Japs on the mainland assume he knows. The fact that his radio has gone for a Burton and they cannot contact him doesn't worry them. The war is over. They are too worried about their own skins to come near a place like this. Remember when the Allies get here this isn't going to be a very healthy place to be in if you're Jap," said Lambert. "Now, any volunteers for the ammunition hut show?"

Everybody volunteered.

"Thanks, chaps. Two it'll have to be. Wilson and Cummings. The others—all of you start a little sing-song in the hut. The other huts will join in. That will keep the Japs on their toes. Make them even more jittery."

"How about sabotaging some Nip trucks?" somebody suggested.

"Or knifing a few of the sentries. . . ?"

Lambert said, very firmly. "No, I only want three men moving outside the huts tonight. And that's too many. I don't want any Errol Flynn-like heroics either. Remember this, if a Jap guard is killed, they'll kill ten or even twenty of our chaps in revenge. That is too high a price to pay."

They grunted in agreement.

"Right. I'm going to scout round Yamamitsu's place. I want to make contact with that girl. She could be useful to us. But the most important show is the ammo hut. So Wilson and Cummings had better slope off first."

He turned to the two officers. "You'll have a fifteen-minute start on me. By the time I leave you should be in position at the ammo hut."

Swinging back to the others he asked, "Any questions . . . ?"

There were no questions.

Chapter Twelve

I

"FASTER! Faster!" Sakamura snapped.

He accompanied his shouts with sharp blows on the neck of the driver in the front seat.

The car was old. The headlamps blinked as it rattled down the rough jungle track. The night was dark, despite the moon, down on the track.

The driver thought that under these conditions he was going too fast already. But he pushed the speed up to forty-five miles an hour.

He feared Sakamura; especially now that he was a Major, and therefore in a position of still more power. Like all the guards he hated Sakamura too; they had a name for him that was a rough translation of a son-of-a-bitch.

The headlamps flickered across tree trunks. The road turned sharply. Ahead the driver could see the lights of the women's camp.

Sakamura peered ahead. Everything seemed quiet in the compound.

The car came to a halt outside the gates. Two sentries shoved rifles through the wiring of the gates. The car driver snapped at them in angry Japanese. The two sentries made no move. They were still jittery after the earlier action.

"It is I, Major Sakamura," shouted Sakamura.

One sentry, thinking himself intelligent, said, "Major Sakamura . . . ? Major Sakamura . . . ?"

He had a feeling that there was something wrong.

Sakamura burst out of the car, pistol in hand. "Who is this diseased son of a one-yen Tokyo whore who dares to question my authority?"

Recognising the newly promoted officer, the guards began to stammer apologies and rushed to open the gates. Sakamura hurried through the gates. Behind him came the four soldiers. The gates swung shut. The two sentries snapped to attention. Sakamura stomped towards them. His face was red with rage.

He came to a stop. He bent forward. "A fine pair," he

snapped. "Donkey waste. The pair of you." His hand came up. He ordered them to tilt their faces sideways. Sakamura balled his fist and brought it down on the first man's cheek.

It made a meaty, thumping sound and the sentry rocked on his feet. Sakamura repeated the performance on the second man, and hit him again. He had been the one who had denied the existence of Major Sakamura.

Sakamura headed for the Administration Block and Captain Sakala. He could see the block was ablaze with lights. They illuminated the bodies, draped with sacking.

There were six.

Sakamura was angry. Angry that Sakala should have taken life without Yamamitsu's or his authority. Clearly, Sakala was not suitable for his job. He abused his powers.

Sakala, Sakamura thought, was nothing more than a sadist.

2

Captain Sakala towered over Kate Keiller. She sat on a wooden stool, her elbows on her knees, her head resting on her cupped hands. There was a bluish bruise on her cheek. No attempt had been made to find her new clothing. She was naked to the waist.

Captain Sakala turned as Sakamura marched in. He began to smile . . .but the look on Sakamura's face killed the smile at birth.

"I am now Major," began Sakamura pompously, in Japanese, for the benefit of the soldiers present. "Colonel Yamamitsu ordered me to investigate the shooting. What happened? Who gave you authority to shoot prisoners under the protection of the Emperor?"

Captain Sakala tried to hide his anger. He knew that he was being made to look foolish in front of his men.

"You are coming to a decision on this matter before you have heard what it is all about," he said.

"I see bodies! I see that gate sentries are nervous."

"There was a murder," Sakala said stiffly, indicating Kate. "This prisoner abused the hospitality of the Japanese Army. She killed a Japanese soldier. Private Hulako, third class. He was but a boy. She lured him to the kitchen with her body. There she stabbed him to death.

"His death was a signal for the other prisoners to break out and try to overwhelm the guards. Only prompt action by my men—under my supervision—saved the situation."

Sakamura scratched his chin.

"I see. I see," he said.

He doubted the story, at least the Captain's version. But he couldn't challenge it unless he had facts to go on. Sakamura knew he would have to look into the story very, very carefully. He wanted to disgrace Sakala. But if he couldn't he knew that Yamamitsu, far from replacing Sakala, would recommend him instead for a medal.

"You had better write a report at once, Captain. Colonel Yamamitsu is waiting. I had better take this woman back to the cells for interrogation. Where are the other witnesses—if there were any."

"One of the Chinese kitchen women, an old woman, knows about it. I have her in the other room. She claims that Private Hulako was in the kitchen and sent her to get this woman—Keiller—the wife of the doctor who escaped. But she is obviously lying. No soldier would do such a thing. She must be questioned carefully."

"I see. Interesting. But it could have happened like that. This simple, good-hearted soldier might have wanted to tell this Keiller woman that her husband was still at large and presumably safe."

"Yes, yes, Major. I never thought of that. Of course it is against regulations. But it is very honourable and human."

"Exactly. But spurning his help this woman"—Sakamura glowered at Kate Keiller—"knifed him."

Sakala nodded agreement. "We try to be kind to them. We want them to become good second-class citizens of Japan. But they not only refuse to co-operate with us, they also try to kill us."

Sakamura lowered his head for a moment before replying to this. "Sakala, you are so right. It is a thankless task. The people back home think we have an easy time of it. So do the soldiers at the front. The prisoners hate us. No, this is no life. I wish for the thousandth time that I had a combat assignment at the front. But some must fight and some must guard."

Sakala agreed.

"I will take the two women. There will be a trial. The crime of killing a Japanese soldier is punished by beheading." Sakamura paused a moment, trying to think when he had last seen a beheading. Too long ago. He needed to see another. But not Kate Keiller. No, not her. He had other plans for her. He looked at the prisoner. She was so composed. So sure of herself. He liked the way her skin looked; tanned and firm. Not like the skin of Japanese women. That was inclined to be yellowish and rather rubbery. He looked again at Kate, a quick look, so that she would not have any idea what he had in mind. But it was a look that took in so much. He saw her well-moulded contours. The firmness of her breasts. The supple thigh muscles. No, she would not die. Not unless she became unco-operative. But Sakamura thought that would be unlikely. He had a firm reputation for dealing with people who were unco-operative. He knew that it was not a particularly pleasant reputation. But it was an effective one.

The Chinese woman would find out soon how effective his reputation was. He had already planned how she would die; he planned it with the consummate care of a chef preparing a banquet. She would be the centre piece in a dish of bloody perversion. Without a doubt, Sakamura thought, she would deny the charge that she had murdered the soldier, had then called Kate Keiller to the hut, so that she would take the blame. But, he smiled, what good were denials?

Sakala saw the smile and buck-toothed one back.

Kate Keiller saw it and shivered. She sensed there was something evil, evil that had been inborn, in the mind of Sakamura. She sensed too that the evil was directed at her.

Sakamura saw her shiver and smiled. She would have no need to be cold in a short while.

"What shall I do with Hulako's body?" Sakala asked.

"What do you think? Eat it? Captain, there is only one thing you can do—bury it quickly," snapped Sakamura distastefully.

Hulako was better dead. A Japanese soldier who could not accomplish the seduction of a woman prisoner without starting a riot, and getting himself killed, had no place in the Imperial Army, or any right to be a Japanese.

Besides, Sakamura was angry with Hulako on other counts. Hulako was a ranker. A country rustic who was little better than the prisoners he guarded. He had no right to try to take a woman who had been marked down for Sakamura.

But even though his mind was made up Sakamura was determined to see if there was any way he could make Sakala lose face.

"Show me the kitchen."

"Of course."

"Arrange for the guards on duty at the time of the incident to be ready for questioning."

"Of course."

Sakamura grunted. He knew that Sakala would fight tooth and nail to keep his post.

"This way, Major," smiled Sakala.

Sakamura smiled. He liked the sound of the word "Major."

3

Mala felt herself slipping into a fitful sleep. The gunfire had stopped. The camp was silent. There was only the odd murmur of voices at the other end of the hut.

The other women were plotting something; Mala thought as she drowsed. The fools. Plotting wasn't for women. Their place was in a house. Especially a bedroom in a house.

She had found that was the best way to live. She had found that it brought the nicer side out in people. Like Captain Sakala. The other woman said he was a stupid bully. But Mala had found him nicer than most of the other women.

The women were strange she thought. They were now openly hostile to her. This hurt Mala, hurt her very much. She didn't want to cause trouble; it had been her constant companion all her life. And yet, since the incident of the chocolates, she sensed that trouble had been mounting over her head.

It broke just as she dropped off to sleep.

That was when the other women came for her.

Arms gripped her shoulder blades, and she moved uneasily.

Then something was rammed down her throat. Something that filled her mouth. Something that sent the blood coursing through her head and set her jaws aching. Something to stop her screaming.

Then she was conscious of the pain that coursed through her body and head as they beat her and scarred her. She felt the blood seeping from a dozen cuts. She felt fingers gouge into her chest. There was more blood trickling down her navel. There were more scratches on her legs.

Then she drifted into unconsciousness. Taking with her the sure knowledge that Captain Sakala would not want to lay in the grass with her anymore.

They hit her with pieces of wood, scratched at her with tins, and pulled tufts of her hair out by the roots.

They made little noise.

They said little.

When they had completed their work they moved back to their beds. They were satisfied.

Kate Keiller, and the dead women, had been avenged.

4

Joe Bellamy knew the parachute was collapsing even as he hit the tree trunk. A branch scratched his face. He bounced sharply against something that did not give. It blasted the breath out of his body.

He had a giddy sensation as he swung to and fro, his feet kicking at air.

He was literally dancing.

He relaxed and waited until the swing had tapered off. He then gently pulled himself up the cords, moving very slowly. But the parachute held. In a moment he reached a branch. As he detached his harness and let it fall, he wondered how far he was from the ground. It was hard to tell in the gloom of the jungle.

He got his legs placed on either side of a thick branch. He began to edge along it. It became very thick, and that suggested to him that he was probably fairly high up in the tree. He swung his back against the trunk, placing his legs comfortably and lit a cigarette.

He had a long wait.

Chapter Thirteen

1

He came down from the tree at first light. He had eaten from his emergency pack, and, checking his compass, he moved off in the direction of the coast.

It was cool moving in the first hours of the day. But when the sun came up, he began to slow down. Then to wilt. He found too, that he was eating far too many of his salt tablets. He would have to ration himself if he wanted to reach the coast.

Soon after noon he stumbled on to the track. He saw the marks. And guessed that it was a road used by the Japanese. He knew that the Anglo-American troops had not penetrated this far. At least not in force.

Bellamy decided to move along the road in the direction of the coast. If he was lucky, and there was no reason why he should not be, he would meet up with the advancing Allies. He was not even greatly disturbed at the prospect of meeting the Japanese.

The war was over.

Everybody was friends again.

"Christ . . ." and Bellamy smiled distastefully. "What a bloody thought. . . ."

They would probably offer him a cigarette and a cup of saki. He swore again.

As he trudged along he wondered what Japanese food would be like. He would demand something special from the vanquished.

That made him smile. For he knew what some of his boys would ask for—Japanese women.

Then he heard the truck.

2

He heard it long before he saw it.

It was an ugly noise in the distance, beating back from the jungle on either side of the track. It was a weak noise, as if the engine was climbing a gradient, and felt that it was an impossible task. Bellamy thought that no truck had ever groaned like this one was groaning.

Bellamy bounded forward. This would be the easy way to travel back to his friends. In a truck, sprawled in the back, relaxed, contented. He started to run towards the noise. He came round a bend in the track and saw the vehicle. It was a Japanese truck all right. It had a large red sun painted on its bonnet. Behind the windscreen he could see the impassive faces of two Japanese soldiers. . . .

Bellamy ran on.

On came the truck. Bouncing and slithering over the ruts and pot-holes.

But the men in the cab did not seem to see Bellamy. He was surprised. . . .

"Slow up . . . slow up." He was almost up to the truck and waving his hand as he shouted.

The men in the cab remained impassive. Now he could see a third face peering at him through a slot window linking the driving cab and the cabin.

Then it happened.

Suddenly. Without warning.

The driver swung the wheel over hard and stepped up his speed as he did so. The truck hurtled towards Bellamy at over fifty miles an hour—its top speed. Had it been able to go faster Bellamy would have been scooped up onto the bonnet and tossed high into the air.

As it was Bellamy had hardly time to move. He saw the heavy metal wheel hub coming straight at him. Above the engine cowling he saw the Japs. They had seen him all right. They were grinning evilly.

Then Bellamy fell away, throwing himself on to the ground, and into the jungle. He heard the shrieks from rubber braking against metal. A pause. Then came the slap, slap of boots padding over the ground.

As he came out of the jungle so they came for him.

Bellamy thought: little Japs. Little goddam Japs who seemed to be everywhere.

He was dazed. He tried to protest. He tried to bluster. But he couldn't raise the breath.

"American murderer!" one of the yellow men bawled.

"We behead you," another snarled, spitting as he did so.

A third grabbed him by the arm.

"You dirty spy," the first one bawled, slapping him hard across the face.

"Confess, confess," snarled the second, also clouting him.

"We really beat you now," smirked the third.

Bellamy tried to protest. He tried to tell them the war was over. But before he could speak they began to beat him. A fist sank into his stomach. A hobnailed boot cracked against his knee. A pistol butt cracked across his forehead.

Ineffectually, Bellamy tried to ward off the blows. His head seemed to explode as the butt descended on the crown of his head. He felt his knees turn to wax and the ground came up and hit him.

He had a momentary impression of being lifted. Rough wooden boards scraped his face as he was dropped on to the floor of the truck.

"You die very soon," said a Japanese voice, gently, as if telling him that there was nothing to worry about. As if he was going home.

The truck moved off.

3

Bellamy thought he could hear a groaning coming from somewhere. Then he realised that it came from within the truck. He tried to open his eyes. But the pain stopped him. He realised he was now on his back, looking up, with the sun boiling down on him. He folded over. The sun still beat down on him. He screamed out for something to shade him from the rays.

Time passed. . . .

The truck lumbered on. Finally Bellamy summoned up enough strength to open his eyes. He saw a guard first. The man had his back to Bellamy. He was leaning forward over the cab, looking along the road.

Bellamy shifted his gaze.

Then he saw the mess. It took him some moments to realise that it was a man. And minutes more to realise that the man was alive. There was blood and grime and bruises on the man's shrunken, half naked body.

Bellamy watched the man. He wanted to vomit. He couldn't realise that this had once been a healthy man. He could not imagine anybody committing such savagery as he had been committed against this man.

As he watched, Bellamy saw his eyes open. They stared about him for a long time. They didn't move. Not even a blink, but the stare of a man who like a zombie, was alive, yet dead. Bellamy thought he was dead, after all; that the opening of his eyes had been a reflex action that often happened when rigor mortis set in.

Then the man's lips moved. Nothing came for a moment. Then the pitiful creature found his voice and Bellamy recognised a cultured English accent.

The voice whispered, "Don't tell them . . . see Colonel . . . Colonel Lambert . . . don't dare tell them the war is over . . they'll kill us . . . kill us . . . far quicker."

"Why . . . why in hell's name should that be?"

"Can't explain . . . tried to get through . . . took some with me . . . no good though . . . they'll kill us . . . once they know it's all over. . . ."

"But——"

There came a scream.

It seemed to come from the sky. Bellamy, not placing it for the moment, tried to roll away.

He saw the boot. He saw it crack against the skull of the Englishman.

Then he placed the scream.

It was a Jap's yell of rage.

He heard the soldier say, as he brutally kicked the Englishman, "No talkee, no talkee. . . ."

Bellamy knew that if the booting hadn't killed the prostrate man, it had certainly ended any hope of more "talkee. . . ."

But he had no time to dwell on this.

The boot turned on him.

"You too no talkee . . . you too quiet. . . ."

The metal-toed boot slammed against Bellamy's head. It was like a bomb going off inside his skull. He felt himself falling. It was like dropping to earth again in his parachute.

If only he could go back to that tree and start again.

Chapter Fourteen

I

THE spider fascinated Lambert. As he lay on his bunk he watched the fat, bloated, incredibly ugly arachnid start to spin a web beneath a crossbeam holding the roof of the hut up. A shaft of watery light, coming through a crack in the roof, spotlit the industrious spider, giving Lambert a crystal view of the insect, as it ran back and forth to spin its delicate structure of gauze.

The spider reminded Lambert of Colonel Yamamitsu.

It had the same fetid odour, though he knew he could not smell the spider—it was just his imagination—it had the same swollen thorax, neck and head.

And it went back and forth beneath that beam, the same way as Yamamitsu went back and forth on his balcony.

And Lambert watched fascinated....

And because he was fascinated the image grew clearer....

The spider's slim, pliable legs, ending in delicate claws became the hands and feet of Yamamitsu; limbs that Lambert had a strong desire to crush and break.

The spider's eyes became the dull, coldly reptilian eyes that Yamamitsu had. Eyes that saw everything, but revealed nothing. The horrible insect exuded slimy liquid from its body in much the same way as Yamamitsu drooled.

And it went back and forth beneath that beam, the same way as Yamamitsu went back and forth on his balcony.

And Lambert watched fascinated....

And because he was fascinated the image grew clearer....

The spider's web took on the pattern of the wire strands surrounding the camp. The web was strong, despite its look of gossamer delicacy. It was strong because it was built well. The spider was a craftsman, each strand was woven with deliberate care. So were the strands of the wire fence surrounding the camp planted with deliberate care.

Each strand of the web radiated from the spider's body.

Yamamitsu's body.

Each strand of the wire surrounding the camp was under his

command. Everything in the camp was under his command. He had spun his web; the victims were chained to him as surely as the victims would be chained to the spider in his gossamer web. The victims in the camp had tried to squeeze and squirm out of the web. But they had only enmeshed themselves more.

And it went back and forth beneath that beam, the same way as Yamamitsu went back and forth on his balcony.

And Lambert watched fascinated. . . .

And because he was fascinated the image grew clearer. . . .

The web was completed. It hung like a suspension bridge over Lambert's bed. It rocked gently when he breathed hot air towards it. But it held. It had been well made.

Now the spider looked around for a victim. It trod across the suspension bridge with purposeful steps.

It was Yamamitsu searching for a prey.

The spider looked down at Lambert. It *knew* it was under observation. He could see its mandibles waving. And as he looked the spider took on a stronger than ever resemblance to Yamamitsu.

And Lambert knew that the Japanese colonel had marked him down as his next victim.

The spider trod on. Its eyes were evil. Its legs were evil. Its body was evil. Then it saw the victim. Trapped at one end of the web. The spider stopped. It slavered. It took its time.

Then it moved on. Slowly, surely, steadily.

The victim made no move. The web was so well made. It waited there. Waited to die. . . .

Lambert knew he could do nothing when Yamamitsu came for him. He would wait for death. . . .

Suddenly the spider slipped. One of its legs became caught in the sticky web. It made an effort to free itself. But it only became more firmly entangled. . . .

But its leg could not support its fat, bloated incredibly ugly body. It rolled off the web. For a moment it was suspended in space by one leg. Then it dropped to the ground.

Lambert watched it fall. And like a man coming out of a nightmare into the clear day he rose from his bed and crushed the spider beneath his feet.

He knew he would have to crush Yamamitsu in the same way.

The knowledge made him feel better. He wiped the sweat off his face. Then he saw the web. It still swung in space. But now it had lost its evil look. Now it seemed harmless.

But Lambert took no chances. In one quick movement he broke the threads. And the victim dropped to the ground and fluttered away. . . .

Lambert looked out of the window.

It was time to go.

2

He slipped from beneath the planking of the hut and wormed his way across the earth. It was the complete darkness of night before the moon rose and there was little chance that he would be seen. But he had to be back before the moon came out.

So had the two men who had gone to sabotage the ammunition store and steal the hand grenades.

They had been gone for some time.

Lambert, moving slowly, stopping every few yards to listen, finally came to the garden of the bungalow. Once it had been cultivated. Once it had been laid out with lush tropical flowers. But now it was a flattened patch, strewn with the rubble and refuse of the bungalow. There were cigarette cartons, tins, and packets.

Lambert took it all in, wrinkling his nose with disgust as he did so.

Then, moving in a crouch, he carefully approached the verandah of the house. He took great care not to disturb the litter that was piled high in his path.

As he lay in the lee of the verandah he heard the sound of music. He recognised it as coming from the gramophone. It was a strange record to hear in such a place and on such an occasion. It was "Pennies from Heaven," and the treacly, maudlin ditty brought a nostalgic twist to Lambert's lips.

He decided against climbing the steps to the verandah. He was afraid Yamamitsu might hear the crunch of his feet on the woodwork. The best way would be to lift himself up on to the verandah direct.

Lambert placed his hands over the top of the verandah. His fingers hooked themselves to the wooden boards. For a minute he made no move. Then gently unbending his knees he slowly brought his head up towards the verandah. It was a movement imperceptible in its slow-motionless. It stopped completely as soon as Lambert's eyes had cleared the level of the verandah. He stared into the darkness of the night; his body, eyes and ears concerted into a listening and watching post.

He became aware of his own danger and helplessness. He wished he had a weapon.

The music came louder. But it was the only sound that disturbed the night.

Lambert inched himself over the verandah. On elbows and knees he wriggled towards the bungalow. Soon he was safe in the deeper shadow of the building.

He saw that one of the windows had been opened. The pane was held back by a hook. The curtain had not been completely drawn and as he crept towards the window Lambert heard Yamamitsu's voice. . . .

"Faster, faster. . . ."

Lambert noticed that the instruction was given in a voice slightly out of breath.

"Yes—yes, master."

It was the voice of the girl. The woman Lambert wanted to find out about. Balling his fists, his face set grimly. Lambert peered through the chink in the curtains.

"Faster . . . faster. . . ."

Lambert saw them then. He saw that Yamamitsu, naked to the waist, was squatting on a cushion in the centre of the room. His back was to the window.

The girl was kneeling beside him, her face to the window. Wisps of spungold hair hung over her forehead as she worked. Her kimono had slipped from her slender shoulders with the repetitive movement she made.

And as Lambert watched, she scooped shampoo lather from Yamamitsu's head and let it drop into a bowl near at hand.

As she did so she looked up at the window.

And she saw Lambert.

She gave a startled sound and drew back. Although there was soap on his forehead and his eyes were closed, Yamamitsu did not miss her gesture.

"What is it, Fair One?"

"Nothing—nothing," she replied, a little too quickly.

Yamamitsu's right hand snaked out and grasped the girl's wrist. His other snatched up a towel to wipe the soap from his face.

"You lie! You saw something! Somebody! Who was it?"

"I saw nothing! It was but a pain in the stomach!"

Lambert dropped beneath the level of the window as Yamamitsu turned to look.

"Which one of the guards was it?" Yamamitsu was angry now. Really angry. "Which one of them was it? I will behead him myself?"

"I saw nothing, nothing," the girl whispered.

Lambert noticed her voice for the first time. It was low, husky, cultured and above all sensual. It was a voice which spoke louder than any gesture she could have made.

He could hear Yamamitsu snarl and the voice repeat that its owner had seen nothing.

". . . this isn't the first time that the guards have spied on me. Nor is it the first time that you have lied to me. Both you and they are in for a lesson!"

Lambert heard footsteps cross the room. He risked a quick look. The girl, her hands clenched to her face, was recoiling in terror.

Yamamitsu, a riding crop in his hand, was advancing on her.

"Who was it?" His voice had a dangerous screech about it. "Which guard was it?"

"There was nobody . . . nobody . . . !"

Yamamitsu was not listening. He had set his mind on punishing the girl, Lambert thought, and any old excuse would serve his purpose. The Jap's arm snaked up and then down, the lash making a swishing sound as it descended.

Lambert felt the pain of that blow as the lash crashed across the girl's shoulders. Then Lambert's eyes strayed inside the room. It was much as he had often seen it in the past. Then his eyes stopped. Glued to a table within easy reach of the window. A small occasional table. A mass produced table. But a very special table now.

There was a gun on it.

Yamamitsu's gun.

And before he could realise it, Lambert had moved. In one conditioned movement he reached through the pane for the gun, cocking his leg over the low sill as he did so.

"Drop that whip, Yamamitsu," said Lambert softly.

The Jap whirled. His mouth sagged open, the cry that came from his throat ended in a squeak.

"*Lambert!*"

Lambert walked slowly towards him, the gun held steadily in his hand.

"So it was you. . . ."

Slowly and deliberately Lambert reached out for the riding crop held in Yamamitsu's paralysed hands. Then like a man in a dream, in a kind of slow-motion, he drew the hand holding the crop back behind his shoulder. Then the spell broke. In one lightning movement he brought the crop slashing across Yamamitsu's face.

The Jap gave a bellow of pain.

Outside the only sound was the chirping of insect life and the rustle of foliage.

"You don't like it, Yamamitsu. Nor do the others who get this treatment."

"Lambert, you will die for this."

"Maybe, but you won't be there to see me die." Once more the lash whipped across Yamamitsu's face. It brought a fresh weal up to join the one that bisected the Jap's cheeks. "It is no good shouting, Yamamitsu, because there is nobody out there to hear you. Save the souls of the men you have killed. They can hear you, and they'll probably enjoy hearing you cry. You had enough enjoyment out of hearing them shriek. . . ."

There was silence in the room.

Then Yamamitsu started to chuckle mirthlessly, "Lambert you are very, very foolish. Unless you shoot me now, you will never kill me. For behind you——"

"There is nothing behind you," said the girl, "It is a trick."

Yamamitsu swore and made a lunge at her. But Lambert was quicker. With a vicious swing he sent the crop crashing across the Jap's eyes. It landed with a noise that sounded like thunder in the confines of the room.

"Never again will you hit her or anybody, Yamamitsu," said Lambert, casually.

The Jap licked his lips. "You cannot kill me in cold blood."

"I can. And I am going to."

"But I have only done my job. War is war."

"Sure war is war. But I'm going to kill you anyway."

I'll kill him when he's suffered. Suffered the same as he made the others suffer. I'll make the fat bastard sweat until he really knows what fear is. Then I'll crush him the same as that spider was crushed. But he's going to suffer, thought Lambert exultantly.

"You will never live long after me," said Yamamitsu.

"Keep trying. It will make no difference!"

"I make you an offer. . . ." Yamamitsu was desperate. "You

leave me now. I promise never to touch you again. I give you many privileges." He looked at the girl. "You can have my woman, Lambert. She very good——"

Lambert hit him once more with the riding crop. "I don't like white women to be talked of like that when there is yellow trash present," he said, softly.

Yamamitsu's face was naked now.

Fear oozed from every pore. And with the fear mingled the sweat and blood. Every flabby contour of his face was full of that fear. Panic was there too. The mind behind the face knew that it had little time left to live.

Lambert laughed at the face, and once more hit it with the riding crop. All the time the girl had made no move. She stood to one side and watched the butchering with a dazed face.

"You cannot shoot me. The noise will bring the guards——"

"But you will never know if they come. Because you will be as dead as the others. Remember Davies. You saw him die. He was a brave man. Not like you. But in a short while you will be as dead as he was. Remember Adams? No, you probably wouldn't. He was just a chopping block for your amusement."

Lambert paused to move the gun more comfortably in his hand. Yamamitsu saw the movement and thought his time to die had come. Sweat bubbled through the blood streaming down his face.

"No, you wouldn't remember Adams. But he had a wife and two children back in my country waiting for him. Did you ever think of them when you ordered him to die? Did you?"

"It—it was war. War is very difficult——"

The lash cut short his words again. Lambert laughed as more blood spattered out of the Jap's wounds. Then in a cold, measured voice he went on.

"No, you didn't care a damn. Do you remember Jenkins. He was a good man. A religious man. He never gave you or the guards any trouble. But you let Sakamura kill him one hot morning to take some of the boredom out of your life."

"No, no, no! It was Sakamura! It was he who was behind it! I did nothing! It was he, he. . . ."

Yamamitsu's voice trailed off as the whip landed once more.

"It is always easy to blame somebody else. But you were the commandant. You were responsible. You will pay for it," Lambert went on remorselessly. "Do you remember Watkins? He was but a boy. And being a boy he was frightened of dying.

He had his whole life before him. He had made plans for his future. He was the only support his widowed mother had. But did you think of any of these things? No! You had him die."

"But—but I did not know——"

"You should have made it your business to find out. And the fact that you did not know is no excuse for murdering people. You killed Watkins in cold blood. And as you will shortly die, try to remember that scream he gave as the bullets hit him. It was not a pleasant sound. I still hear it now in my sleep. But I shall not hear your scream when I sleep."

"Please, please, Lambert. . . ."

Lambert smiled. He had never had such a good time as he watched the Jap squirming. He enjoyed the way Yamamitsu's hands shook, the way his mouth wobbled, the way the blood streamed down his face.

"There were others, Yamamitsu. There was that young soldier from Belfast. You do not even know what his name was, and if you did, it would mean nothing to you. But Partingdon wanted to live. As they all wanted to live. But what did you do? Nothing! You enjoyed it as they were massacred."

Lambert paused to wipe the sweat trickling down his nose. But his eyes never left Yamamitsu.

"You might remember Young. He had courage. More courage than all you and your guards have put together. He was a big man. And like all big men he had a surprising way of being able to move quickly. And you should remember how he moved when they took him out to dig his grave . . . for you were there the whole time. You didn't like Young, did you? He was too big for you. When you or the guards hit him it seemed to have no effect. You couldn't take that, could you, Yamamitsu? It made you feel what you are—a dirty little bastard. So when Young charged the gunners you were happy to see the bullets crash him to the ground. At last he had been cut down to size. But Young was a friend of mine and for that too you must suffer."

With that Lambert sent the whip criss-crossing across Yamamitsu's face until it was a blubbery mass.

"Why . . . why you torture me?" The Jap's voice had taken on a pathetic squeak.

"Because I hate your guts. Because of what you have done to the others. You enjoyed torturing them. See how you like it now."

Yamamitsu was hysterical now. His control had completely

gone. "I will do anything . . . anything . . . let me live, please et me live."

Lambert laughed. A hard, humourless laugh.

"To hell with that, Yamamitsu, you have to die. And I think the time has come."

Yamamitsu started to quiver. Then suddenly he was charging Lambert. A blind, bull-like charge.

Lambert moved fast.

He raised the gun and clubbed the Jap behind the ear. Yamamitsu skidded across the floor on his devastated face. But incredibly he rose and charged once more, grunting and reeling as he did so. Lambert hit him a mighty wallop in the stomach. He felt his fist sink deep into layers of flesh.

Then his hands were firmly round Yamamitsu's neck. He increased the pressure and in one smooth movement jerked the Jap off his feet.

They fell heavily to the floor. Lambert straddled the man, banged his head against the floor several times, then jerked backwards.

Yamamitsu was still on the floor when Lambert caught him squarely in the groin with his boot. The Jap jack-knifed, and rolled over on to his side.

Lambert was not finished. He dropped on to the Jap and once more applied pressure to his throat. Yamamitsu looked at him. His eyes were popping out like polished plastic buttons. His mouth sagged wide. And blood flowed everywhere, especially down his throat.

On the gramophone a sleepy-voiced singer was singing . . . "Stop, stop, darling, and let me breathe."

Yamamitsu made a desperate attempt to shake Lambert off. He clawed and scratched at the Englishman. But Lambert, like a bulldog, held on. And as he did so he murmured, "Any second now, Yamamitsu, any second now. And as you go take with you the knowledge that the war is over . . . that was why we sabotaged your radio and other equipment. We knew you would kill us once you knew the war was over. That was why you had to die first . . . and it is now the time."

Lambert gave a last powerful squeeze.

And quite suddenly Yamamitsu was still. His body seemed to relax. His eyes, still staring at Lambert, became vacant and unmoving.

Lambert heard a stifled gasp from somewhere behind him and the girl whispered, "You've—you've killed him."

"Yes."

"We'll be shot for this—or worse."

Lambert smiled. A gentle and tired smile. "Not if I can do anything about it." Now that it was all over Lambert felt terribly tired. But he knew there were still things to do. First he had to hide the body. But even when that was done, there was still the fact that it would only delay the inevitable: Yamamitsu would be missed in hours. Then would come the revenge.

Then he saw the bowl of prawns. And the idea started to gell.

He turned to the girl and said, "Clean up his face. Quickly!"

She detected the urgency in his voice and using the shampoo bowl wiped away the blood and sweat with a sponge. She threw the blood-stained water and sponge out of the window.

Meanwhile Lambert had picked up the prawn dish. He selected a large prawn from the treacly brown liquid they floated in. Kneeling he scattered the rest of the prawns over the carpet. Then he poured the treacly brown liquid over Yamamitsu's face. It effectively hid the weals caused by the lashing. Then he placed the prawn bowl just out of reach of the Jap's outstretched hand. Finally, carefully prising Yamamitsu's teeth apart, he pressed the prawn firmly into his throat.

The girl said, softly. "It will look as if he choked. . . ."

"I hope so. I hope that Sakamura will not look too closely. But he probably won't. He will be far too pleased at the prospect of taking over from Yamamitsu."

"Maybe. But they will question me."

Lambert smiled and said, "No they won't. Because you won't be here. . . ."

"But——"

"We will hide you. I know the very place."

"But they will search for me."

Lambert had an idea. He saw the pistol holster and pistol and riding crop. And he quickly gathered them up. He put the crop back in its proper place. Then turning to the girl he said, "When you have cleared away traces of the fight gather a haversack and fill it with tins of food and milk. Leave others scattered about. We must give the Japs the impression that you've fled from the camp."

"But they will suspect. How could I ever leave the camp?"

"By the fencing at the end of the garden here. This is the easiest point to break out of because the prisoners are not allowed up here."

"I see. . . ."

The decision was made. Lambert snapped into top gear to carry it out.

"Hurry then. The food. Get a tin opener. This is not just to fool the Japs. You'll need it anyhow, where you are going."

She left. Lambert, pistol in hand, searched the desk. He looked through a pile of documents and newspaper clippings. They were written in Japanese. He could not understand a word.

He found three spare clips of pistol ammunition and thrust them in his pocket. He found a compass, and took it. When the girl came back, Lambert was ready to go. He took the haversack from her and threw it over his own shoulder. Then, taking her by the hand, he hurried out on to the verandah and across the garden.

The moon had not risen yet. But Lambert knew there was little time to spare.

They reached the end of the garden and started to crawl.

3

They approached the prisoners' assembly hall very carefully. Then they made their way round to the back of the building. Lambert listened for long minutes. All was quiet.

His hand reached up for a board. The board swung free from the wall, bringing with it a section of the wall which opened just wide enough for a body to pass through.

They passed through the gap and Lambert pulled the wall back into place behind them. They were beneath the dais in the hall.

The men who had sweated and died to build this hall had improvised this hiding place. They were not sure why they had done so. But somebody had said it might "be a good thing." So it had been done.

"I'm afraid it is going to be very dark in here. But it is dry and quite safe." He squeezed her hand to give her encouragement. "There are only four officers who know about it," he explained.

The girl crawled in and Lambert followed. In the darkness he had to feel for the girl. He caught her by the arm and whispered, "This way." He took her to a corner and lowered the haversack.

"I don't know how long you will be here. But I can tell you that the position is not hopeless. We are expecting release at any time."

The girl gripped him by the arm. Her breath caressed his face. "I'm frightened. It's so dark in here," she whispered.

"Nothing to worry about. There are men, friends, all around you. You will hear them moving about in the hall and thumping on the stage. Their language will be very strong at times, but there is nothing I can do about that."

Lambert sensed that she smiled at that.

"And I will try to get in and see you."

"Each day," she pleaded.

"It is possible . . . if I can't get away I'll send somebody else. . . ."

"I'd rather you came than anybody else. . . ."

"I'll try."

Her grip tightened on his arm and she sobbed softly. "It is so long . . . so long since I have spoken to my own people . . . I could sit and talk all night. . . ."

"What's your name. I hate having to address you without knowing whom I am talking to."

She told him—Evaline Kennedy. And then she told him a little about herself. Her father had been a bank manager in Singapore. The Japanese had locked him in the bank vaults until he had suffocated. She didn't know where her mother was. But she had been taken to a Japanese brothel. There Yamamitsu had met her. Then she had been posted to Blood Island. She had been transferred shortly afterwards to the women's compound on the island. Then had come the morning Yamamitsu had picked her out. . . .

"It's all over now," said Lambert gently. "You will soon be away from here."

Then he kissed her gently on the forehead and left.

When he got back to his hut he found the senior officers waiting for him.

They had thirty hand grenades in a blanket on the bed. The raid on the ammunition hut had been successful and had gone without a hitch.

Chapter Fifteen

I

THEY were not the only ones who left their huts to vanish into the darkness. But unlike Lambert and the two who had gone to the ammunition huts the others had no set task that had been approved and blessed by the senior prisoners. Rather, they went for a variety of reasons, all of which were unofficial. They went without telling anybody.

Some were frightened to tell in case they were ordered not to go. Others did not tell in case they failed in what they had set out to do, and failure was a hard thing to live with in a prison camp. Some thought that by not telling they would minimise the repercussions which would follow if they were caught.

Some were foolish; some were calculating, as far as they could be calculating in a situation where the risks were immense and the rewards pitifully few; some were dedicated, not dedicated in the accepted sense. Not the dedication that comes by single-mindedness of purpose, the dedication that belongs to a priest or a doctor bent on doing good in a spiritual and physical sense. No, the dedication that belongs in a prison camp; the dedication of men who had nourished plans, schemes, hopes, fears and other emotions until they had become too strong to live with; too overpowering to be resisted; too demanding to be refused.

All believed they were right in what they were doing. They felt that was a good enough reason for doing what they hoped to accomplish.

Making a decision in a prison camp is not a hard one. The issue is simple. The person making the decision asks, in effect, will he benefit or suffer *personally* by the decision he takes? Again the benefit to be gained by any decision is a limited one. For there are only limited things for a prisoner of war to benefit from. The first one is Freedom.

Freedom.

A simple word. A meaningless word to all those who accept it as part of their daily heritage. The freedom to walk where they choose. The freedom to think, to speak, to choose their own form of employment and amusement. Yet that word, that simple, meaningless word, has caused wars to be fought, empires to fall. On a more personal scale, it has split families, turned father against son, daughter against mother.

Every prisoner sprinkles his conversation with freedom. They talk of the day they will be free; what they will do when they are free; what they had done before their freedom was taken from them. For many that word has become a cross; to bear, to accept, but never to discard. For when a prisoner discards his hope for freedom then he has discarded his hope of living.

No man or woman, confined against their will, can afford to do that. It is the main thing that sustains them.

After freedom comes food.

No prisoner is satisfied with the food he gets. Either its quality is poor or there is not enough of it. On Blood Island both conditions applied.

When they were not thinking of freedom, the men and women immured there thought of food. They looked at the skin drawn tightly against their bones, and they knew that only food, good, nourishing food, not the gruel slop they lived on, would hide those bones with flesh. They did not want lavish food; there was no dreaming of sumptuous meals; rather, it was a longing for a bellyful.

And after food came a desire for relaxation. Despite the wide field that word covered, their ideas of relaxation were limited and practical. A hot bath. A seat in the stalls. Good English beer, straight from the barrel. A song and dance in the local. And little else. For those things were the strongest memories they had of the life they had lived before their freedom had been taken from them. And only the strongest memories could survive the conditions of Blood Island.

So when they went out into the darkness; the foolish, the calculating, the dedicated; they took with them those precepts. Not in their conscious mind. For there was no room in their conscious mind for anything save how to avoid being spotted until they had succeeded in what they were going to do. But these things were in a corner of their mind; they acted as a subtle reminder that if they succeeded they might allow them to return to their conscious mind. That once again, freedom, food and amusement would be theirs without the asking.

2

Archer was the first to go.

He had listened as Lambert had outlined his plans. He had stood at the fringe of the circle surrounding the senior officer. But even there, he did not feel he belonged.

The men around Lambert were all soldiers; professionals who had chosen a way of life that was geared, indeed was the be-all and end-all, to action in its most violent form. They were men who were prepared to die and to let others die because it was the very essence of their life.

Archer felt that he was like them in only one respect. He would have no compunction about letting a man die—providing he was guilty. Providing that he had been tried fairly in a public court. Providing that a Judge had summed up in an objective and careful manner. Providing that a jury had returned a proper and just verdict. If that verdict was guilty, Archer would have no remorse about it. In the way that a physician has no remorse when a patient died after every possible attempt had been made to save his life.

Archer had prosecuted and defended, with equal success, men and women who had been on trial for their lives. Whatever side he was on he had approached each case, each life, with the cold, dispassionate logic of a barrister. He had never allowed emotion to influence him, and he had never used emotion. It was something that he looked on as a sign of weakness, to be treated with grave distrust. He knew that juries could be swayed by emotion. He had seen other counsel sway them with powerful rhetoric. But he knew too that in the long run, in the final balance, it was facts which counted.

Soldiers didn't need facts. They were no part of their armoury. Their task was to kill. Kill quickly, if possible, cleanly; to kill with the minimum loss of life to those who did the killing. Facts were for the politicians. To twist, to use for propaganda. But not for the soldiers, and those who commanded them. Soldiers did not have to rely on a legal system to kill. They saw a man, a platoon, a target—and they tried to wipe it out. It was as simple as that. And after one target had been destroyed, the soldiers looked for another one. And another one after that. War was nothing more than one target after another. The men who did the killing had no real thoughts about it. It was an impersonal business. It was their life blood.

But as Archer had listened to Lambert; listened to his quiet, measured tones that carried so much authority and would have been at home in the High Courts, he had felt, suddenly and without definite reason, that maybe they were right and he was wrong.

After Lambert had finished his briefing, Archer had lain on his bed and analysed every word of what the senior officer had said. And as he had thought about the words, the conviction had grown that Lambert was right, especially under the circumstances.

Once Archer had accepted this—and with the acceptance had come the realisation that he was wrong—he had wondered what he could do. His mind said—NOTHING. He was a lawyer, not a killer. But his emotions, those nervous reactions he kept under careful lock and key, gnawed at his mind. They said: DO SOMETHING.

It was as simple as that.

For an hour Archer had lain on his bunk and asked himself: DO WHAT?

And in the darkness, the comfortable darkness, the idea had been born.

Lambert had said there was to be no killing. No knifing of the guards. He had said the risk was too great. That there would be reprisals. But supposing a Jap was killed and there would be no reprisals on the prisoners because nobody would know how the soldier had died.

Supposing....

Archer knew it could be done. There were ways of killing a man without showing how it had been done. In his long years at the criminal bar he had heard many a prosecution tale of murder which had been done skilfully and cleanly. There had been the case of *Rex v. Kemp*; he remembered it well. He had appeared for the defence. It had been an easy case. Kemp had been charged with the murder of an old man. But the prosecution failed to show how he had done it. The jury had acquitted after a short retirement.

But Archer knew how Kemp had done it....

And the barrister felt he could use the same method to dispose of a Japanese guard, and return to his hut without anybody knowing.

Once the decision was made he felt relieved. He knew that Lambert would forbid him to go. But Lambert need never know, just as the prosecution had never known in the Kemp case.

It had been easy getting out of the hut. The others were all at the far windows looking towards the ammunition hut or the bungalow. Archer had gently opened a window at the far end of the room and in a moment he was through it.

He looked back. He could see the less intense blackness that marked the window. He moved away a couple of yards, and the less intense blackness vanished. He paused to get his bearings. Everything had seemed so clear in the daytime. Now it was all so indistinct and confusing.

He looked back once more.

The building was a hazy blur. He felt suddenly cold, though the night was warm and humid. He shivered slightly in his drab garb.

He knew where he was making for. The wire fence. At irregular intervals guards patrolled the fence. It would be easy to creep up on one . . . and using the Kemp method kill the guard. It would be easy. . . .

It had seemed easy when he had picked holes in the prosecution case.

But now?

Now, he wasn't so sure. It was so lonely out in the compound. No cover. Nothing save the hard-baked ground to hide him.

He started to crawl. The ground seemed even harder and rubbed painfully on his hands and knees.

Away to his left dark buildings loomed up. They were store rooms, used only in the day time. There was nothing to fear from that quarter.

Everything was quiet.

Too quiet.

But so far everything had gone without a hitch. He must have been a funny sight to anybody who could see him; a grown man crawling along the ground like a baby making its first movements.

Suddenly he saw him.

He was standing about ten yards away. Right in his path. An armed sentry!

Archer pressed his body hard into the ground. He felt sure he could hear his heart thumping. He bit his tongue and pinched his palms to control his panic. He wondered if this was a trap. Whether the Japanese had known all along that he was about to set out and kill one of them. Were they just waiting for him to come and shoot him down as he crawled by.

The guard stamped his feet on the ground. To Archer it sounded like the hooves of horses. Then the sentry turned round. Archer could make out the greyish-yellow of his face. It was a young face, a stupid one, a typical Japanese face. Ugly, Mongolian, hard.

He was looking straight at where Archer was lying. He buried his face to the ground and bit still harder on his tongue. He heard footsteps. He stopped breathing. The steps were moving away. He looked up.

It was a fatal thing to do.

The sentry swirled round, casting anxious looks to left and right; his long-barrelled rifle made even longer by the twelve-inch bayonet attached to its muzzle.

Archer saw every contour on his face; the flattened nose, the high cheekbones, the wide, sloping forehead. He tried to crawl away, knowing that he had been seen, but somehow feeling that crawling would minimise the discovery.

The sentry started to grin. A wide and wolfish grin. Then his heavy boots started to thud over the ground. Archer looked up. The Jap stood less than three feet away, his bayoneted rifle held high for the down thrust.

They looked at each other for a flitting of time; the gentle and the savage; the killer and the about to be killed. Archer knew no fear. He felt nothing as he lay there, staring up at the tip of the bayonet. He felt vaguely disappointed that he had not managed to emulate Kemp, but that was all. But his mind was working even if his emotions had frozen. Before he knew it he had gathered himself up, using his knees as a springboard and was raising himself up to leap at the Japanese when the bayonet came down.

Archer saw the guard's left foot rise off the earth to give added power to his downward thrust. He tried to jerk sideways. He put his hands in front of him to ward off the blow.

But the bayonet passed between his hands. It struck him in the throat, passed through his windpipe and came out between his shoulder blades.

Archer died quickly if not cleanly.

3

Parsons, the soldier of fortune, had always wanted to escape since the day he had arrived at Blood Island. Since Sheppey's execution he sensed that the time had come to make his bid. All his life Parsons had been in tight corners. All his life he had wriggled out of them at the last moment.

That moment had now come.

Parsons had seen the excitement down at the main gates. He had watched Sakamura and his escort drive away from the camp towards the spot where the shooting had come from. He had watched the confusion among the remaining sentries. And he knew he could turn that confusion to his own ends.

His plan was simple. He was going through the wire. Somehow, he had obtained a rusty wire cutter; Parsons had a knack of getting things like that. His was a plan which could easily succeed because it was so simple. Besides he had neither the tools or time to make an elaborate tunnel exit from the camp. Once free he planned to strike for the mainland. He was confident that in the jungle he would be more than a match for any pursuit. He had spent some time in the swamps of Indo-China; a training which had hardened him to the rigours of primitive life.

Parsons told his plans to Adams, his only friend in the camp. Adams was a small, wiry man with a brutal face. But he was a prisoner and the idea of escape appealed to him immensely. He begged Parsons to let him go along.

Shortly after Archer had left his hut, the two men sneaked out of theirs.

The pair made straight for the wire.

Away at the main gate the searchlight blinked on, cutting a swathe of light into the darkness. For a moment it wavered then it swung round, skimmed over one hut, then another, and finally settled on the hut Parsons and Adams had left. For long moments the beam stayed steady.

By then the two men had reached the wire. Working steadily, for speed can produce panic under such circumstances, Parsons snipped through one strand after another.

Then the searchlight beam swung away from the hut. Like a

mechanical hound it sped across the ground, almost as if it was sniffing after the tracks of the two men.

On it came. A relentless yellow spotlight. Probing for something that it knew it must find; almost as if it had a sort of sixth sense about the matter. On it came. . . .

Then Parsons was through the wire. The barbs had scratched and torn at his body; he was bleeding profusely. Adams was crawling through the strands when the beam reached the fence.

It sped over the wire until it came to the severed part. Then it seemed to go wild. It jerked up and down, went from side to side in its excitement.

Adams was caught like a moth in a flame. The soldiers running towards him could see every wrinkle of fear in his sweating, trembling face.

Then the beam lifted over the wire, and picked out Parsons. Twice he zigzagged, but the searchlight clung to him. He hadn't a chance.

Two shots rang out.

The escape bid was over.

4

Solman had planned his escape with psychological care, as was to be expected of him. He had sat for several hours after Sheppey's execution, mulling over the situation. He had finally decided that the best psychological time to make an attempt would be in the hours of darkness following the execution.

He reasoned, not without some logic, that the hours of darkness would be the best time. The Japanese would know that the prisoners would be dog-tired after being up all the previous night to witness the mock trial and its aftermath. They would assume after Sheppey's death nobody would feel tempted to make a break for it.

It was all very logical and plausible. Any text-book on psychological reactions would have used the same premise.

But Solman did not know that the Japanese had time for neither logic or plausibility. They had, what Osbert Heinemann had once called "the Oriental approach to being human and happy." Solman should have known better: Heinemann was one of the great popular psychologists in the 1930's.

But he analysed the position and decided to go. He

approached Doctor Smith, the quack medicine salesman. The doctor listened gravely to what Solman had to say, nodded his head sagely and agreed that it was a sound psychological time to go.

But they were not sure how they would make the bid.

They finally decided that the best thing would be to get to the wire fence and see what transpired. After all, as Solman said, the psychological situation might change considerably by the time they reached the fence and they would have to adapt their plans to meet its requirements.

5

Private (Fourth Class) Yashid Lamoo squatted in the lee of the fence and cursed his luck. He was forty, a small tubby man, with a receding hairline and, unusual for a Japanese, he had a bushy moustache. Coupled with the rimless spectacles he wore, the overall impression was of a mandarin.

As he sat there self-pity coursed through his body and mind. He had been roused from bed to take over guard duty when the regular guards had joined Sakamura's posse heading for the women's compound. Lamoo had grumbled about it. Then his guard corporal had roughly told him to keep quiet, and had said that Lamoo's next leave was cancelled.

He had laughed ironically at that. There was nowhere to spend his leave on Blood Island, save the women's compound. And that didn't interest Lamoo. For women were no part of his life.

The other guards disliked him for this. He was a figure of fun and derision.

All his adult life he had been a figure of fun and derision. In Tokyo the waiters at the restaurant he worked in had jeered at him. So had the women in his street. Even his family had looked on him as an oddity. Yet he gave no trouble. He never foisted himself on to those who had no desire to join him. He was a lonely old man; a reprobate full of self pity and frustration.

He had squatted on his buttocks since dusk. It had been a boring time. Nothing had happened along his part of the wire. He had been given the loneliest part of the fence to watch. It was at the far end of the camp, away from the huts and main gate. Even the searchlight could not reach his part of the wire.

As he sat there he lit yet another cigarette. Smoking on duty was strictly forbidden. Sakamura had said that any escaping prisoner would see the glowing butt and would steer clear. Lamoo had used a very terse four letter word when he had read the instruction. Smoking was one of the vices he could not keep down.

With great deliberation he lit a cigarette, flipped away the match into the darkness and cuddled his rifle. He must have smoked half of the cigarette when he heard the noise.

He acted swiftly for a tubby man.

He crushed the butt out in the palm of his hand, oblivious to the pain. Then, in one clean movement he was on his stomach, facing into the compound, rifle at the ready.

He heard the noise again.

He pressed his ear to the ground and tried to locate the sound. At the same time his mind said: this could be your chance. Now you can show the others that you are as smart as they are. Then they will accept you.

He listened for a long moment. The noise had stopped. But before it had stopped it had sounded quite close. And even as he listened it started again. A slow, snakelike, slithering towards the fence, away on his left.

His eyes shifted in that direction. He saw the silhouettes of two humps moving across the ground. The humps moved a few feet and dropped. Lamoo cocked his ears. He could make out the harsh wheeze of air being forced into lungs that were not used to exercise.

In that moment he made his mind up. In one movement he jerked his rifle up and fired.

The report sounded thunderous in the still of the night.

A split second later Lamoo fired again. His second shot drowned out the scream which had followed the first one. He only heard the scream of pain and fear which filled the air after the second report had died away.

He lumbered towards the humps. He reached the first one, and using his boot as a lever, turned it over. It was Solman. A few yards behind him lay the doctor.

Both had been shot through the head.

There was no more firing that night. There were no more attempts to escape either.

Chapter Sixteen

I

SAKAMURA bundled Kate Keiller into his car. Then he turned to Captain Sakala and smirked, "I have made my investigation and it would not be proper for me to discuss it with you." Sakamura was enjoying himself. Let Sakala worry about what he would tell Yamamitsu. "I suggest that you write a report on what happened at once."

The captain nodded and saluted. It was a most military salute.

Sakamura was pleased it was. He liked to see his men and officers displaying military efficiency. He indicated the old kitchen woman, being held by two soldiers. He did not want her in his car.

"Supply immediate transport for that hag, captain," ordered Sakamura, climbing into the car beside the driver. In the rust-flecked driving mirror he could see Kate Keiller huddled in the rear seat; a pathetic, forlorn piece of human flotsam. With a crash of gears the car lurched away from the Administration Block. The sentries at the gate yanked opened the gate, saluting at the same time. The sight brought a smile to Sakamura's lips.

Then out of the camp, the car picked up speed. As it did so Sakamura turned and looked speculatively at Kate Keiller. Her tattered dress was invitingly tight against her body. Head in hands, she sat quite still. She was not weeping, nor moving. She seemed to be in some kind of daze.

And as Sakamura thought about her his mind was made up. She was too good to die. He would fix his report. She would be grateful for that, or should be anyway. And in return . . . ?

In return . . . ?

It brought a thin smile to his lips. Of course he would have something in return. He would have her. It was as simple as that. He had saved her from being executed. From losing her head. And in time, maybe she would grow to like the idea. Sakamura was a practical man. He knew that he couldn't expect her to accept him at once. But there would be ways. . . .

Just as Yamamitsu had found a way to make his woman accept him.

The thought of Yamamitsu wiped the smile off his face. He knew the colonel would not like the idea of Sakamura taking a white geisha. He would enforce the dislike by quoting some obscure Army regulation. But Sakamura was determined, in a polite way, to tell his colonel to go to hell. He knew too that taking Kate Keiller might create a personal problem for Yamamitsu. He had had his present geisha for some time. He might well be tiring of her. The sight of Kate Keiller could well bring the fact over to him. Sakamura thought that his colonel might take her over, claiming it was his right as the senior man. And again, Sakamura decided he would tell his colonel to go to hell if that should arise. Rather than part with the woman he would execute her.

He looked at Kate Keiller and smiled again. He hoped he would not have to kill her . . . not yet, anyway. . . .

As the car sped towards the men's camp, he made his plans. He would accuse the Chinese woman first. But if Yamamitsu showed any interest in Kate Keiller he would have no hesitation in implicating her in the killing, saying that she had blamed the old woman. Sakala's report would give added weight to this. Yamamitsu would have no alternative but to allow Kate to die.

Sakamura looked at her again. If she had to die, he would behead her himself. The thought of cutting off such a pretty head sent a faint shiver of pleasure through his scrawny body. But it would be far better the other way. . . .

He lit a cigarette. Then, puffing a cloud of smoke out of his mouth and nostrils he turned towards Kate Keiller.

She shivered.

"There is nothing to fear. I am your friend."

She lifted her head and looked at him fleetingly, then turned away.

"I will see you do not suffer. I am so sorry that the stupid soldier attacked you. If you had not killed him, I would. He deserved to die," droned Sakamura.

Kate cringed away from his hand, roaming over her leg. She moved her leg, but his hand followed. He looked at her for a moment then whispered, "Do you wish to live . . . ?"

She nodded her head dumbly. She could think only of her husband, in the jungle, alone, trying to bring help. She must live for him.

"Good. I am so pleased," purred Sakamura, "But you must

do as I ask you. Will you obey me in all things otherwise I cannot save you."

She nodded again.

"It is very serious crime you have committed. It will take much work on my part to save you from death."

"I will do anything you want," she whispered.

He smiled and his hand increased its pressure on her leg. He could hardly speak. But he croaked an order for the driver to stop the car.

Kate Keiller knew what was to happen. But she made no protest. She prayed that her husband would understand when she told him.

The car came to a stop. Sakamura turned to the driver and said, "You walk back to camp. I left my gloves in Captain Sakala's office. Gloves very important to me. Quickly, quickly. . . ."

The driver bowed. His face was a mask. He walked away. But when he had gone some way he grinned. He knew that Sakamura had no gloves with him.

He paused for a smoke when he saw a pair of headlamps approaching in the distance and the sounds of a lorry approaching.

2

Sakala stomped back to his office after Sakamura left. Outside the office door was a sentry. A stupid, ox of a man. Sakala couldn't strike Sakamura but he could take it out on the sentry.

He stopped before him and glared. "You pig!" he screamed.

The man turned large cow-like eyes on Sakala. He bowed deeply.

"You filthy pig!"

The man nodded. He bowed again. As he came up Sakala cuffed him once and walked into his office. He settled behind his desk to draft out the report to Yamamitsu.

Hardly had he started to write when he heard the sound of an engine.

He felt a momentary fear; Sakamura must have returned to humiliate him further. Then he recognised the note of the engine. It was that of a truck.

Sakala hurried out to meet it. He went eagerly, all thoughts of the report gone from his mind. It might well be a fresh batch fo prisoners. That could mean, young, healthy women.

Sakala was tiring of Mala.

He reached the gates as the truck stopped.

Soldiers climbed out of the truck.

"You have prisoners . . . ?"

The soldiers saluted and the oldest one said, "Two, Captain."

"Good. Let me see. Let me have a good look," said Sakala, rubbing his hands.

"They are for the men's camp, Captain."

For a minute Sakala did not understand. "What you mean, the men's camp? Who wants them? On whose orders do women go to the men's camp? Speak! Answer me!"

"Captain, they are men prisoners."

"Then why stop here?"

The soldier bowed and said, "To tell you, Captain, that we have recaptured the escaped prisoner, the doctor named Keiller."

"So . . . ? Very good!"

Sakala was surprised. But Yamamitsu would be pleased. He would stage a double execution; husband and wife dying together. It would be quite a novelty.

He was about to say something when he detected a movement from the rear of the truck. Then he saw a man totter from the truck and stagger towards the women's huts, croaking something that sounded like, "Kate . . . Kate!"

That would be Keiller, Sakala decided. The man looked half dead. But what could he expect? Nobody had asked him to escape.

Keiller had dropped to the ground. His mind was aflame with fever, his body ached from the blows he had received.

Sakala snatched a Tommy-gun from the arm of one of the gawking men and fired a short burst into the back of Keiller's head. There was only a red smear on the ground where the doctor's head had lain. Turning to the soldiers, Sakala said, "He tried to escape. He was dangerous. . . ."

The guards nodded and agreed that he tried to escape. . . ."

From the rear of the truck Bellamy had seen the shooting. He felt a great sense of despair and sank back on to his haunches.

Sakala returned to his office. He felt happy. He felt he wanted to be entertained. He ordered a guard to bring Mala to his office. . . .

He sat and waited, smiling as he smoked. The guard returned. Alone. In a guttural voice he reported that the prisoner, Mala Byeong, was dead.

3

Sakamura drove the car through the gates of the men's camp. He felt contented and relaxed. Behind him came the truck, holding the American pilot. Sakamura smiled. He was in for a busy time. There was the maid to question, then the pilot. Kate Keiller would also have to go into the cell block with the others. But that was a mere formality. He would instruct the guards to treat her well.

But before all this he would have to report to Colonel Yamamitsu.

4

Sykes turned over on his bunk and sniffed. Then he jerked into wakefulness. He had heard the sound of a car and truck crossing the compound. He called out to Dawson.

"What is it?"

"Somebody playing silly sods."

"Bastards woke me."

"Go back to sleep."

"I can't."

"Well, shut up."

Sykes rolled on to his back and grunted.

5

Lambert heard the car and truck. He was seated on his bunk. Around him sat the senior officers.

The only light in the hut came from the moon. It touched the faces of the circle of men. It made them look ghostly white, grim, determined, tight of lip.

An officer crossed to the window and watched the two vehicles stop at Yamamitsu's house. He saw several people get out and enter the bungalow. It was impossible to identify them, but the officer thought one of the men was Sakamura.

"I wonder what suffering he has inflicted on those poor women?" said Father Anjou.

Lambert nodded briefly and went on with what he had been saying. . . .

". . . We must be prepared for a showdown. The Japs will be ripe for one. The only chance we have is to get in first. Surprise is our only hope."

Several voices murmured agreement.

"Yamamitsu is dead. Without doubt Sakamura will take over. He's an even bigger bastard, begging your pardon, padre, than Yamamitsu was. Now what will he do!" Lambert might have been taking a briefing for a military attack on some complicated objective. "I think he will do one of two things. Either he will turn all his guards on us at once. Or he will wait and butcher us off in small groups.

"Whatever way it goes, it is going to be damned unpleasant for us. Sakamura, as we all know, is a past master at the finer arts of finger pulling and so on. He will be running this place until the Allies arrive. That might be some while yet. And if Sakamura gets an idea that rescue is at hand I think he'll knock us all off just like that." Lambert flicked his fingers.

"I take it, sir, that you think we should have a crack first—and quickly," said an officer.

"Correct."

"It could mean that a lot of the prisoners could be hurt or killed," warned Father Anjou. "And the outcome would be the massacre of the women and children."

"If we wait, that will come anyway," said Lambert.

"That is only a surmise," reasoned Father Anjou. "We must not take the Japanese too much at their word. Because they have used violence towards us, does not mean that they will wipe us all out just like that." He imitated Lambert's finger flick.

"I think it does, padre," said Lambert, softly. "I am sure that they dare not let us live. With our evidence, they could expect short shrift from the Allies. Don't forget, that with us alive, we could put the rope round Sakamura and his thugs' necks."

"Maybe . . . maybe you are right. But what do you plan to do?" asked Father Anjou.

"Simply this. We have hand grenades. I have one pistol. Some of the men have rough, hand-made weapons. We use that as the basis for getting some real weapons."

"When . . . ?"

"Padre, it will be as soon as possible," said Lambert.

"There are forty guards," somebody said.

"At this camp alone. Probably the same number at the women's place."

"And once the shooting starts, they'll come tailing down here."

"It'll take some while."

"It'll also take some time for us to beat the lot down here."

"Depends on how quick we are."

"Yes . . . if we haven't overpowered the guards here by the time the others arrive, we will be finished anyway," said Lambert.

"But what are your plans?" asked Father Anjou, firmly.

"We have a hundred good men we can rely on. Right?" Lambert looked at the intelligence officer.

"Right, sir."

"Well, they must be briefed."

"Briefed, sir?" The intelligence officer sounded horrified. "Do you intend to let a hundred men in on the plans for the show."

"No, man, of course not!" Lambert was getting exasperated at the continual interruptions. "Can I go on now, and you all listen?"

Everybody, nodded.

"Right. This is the score, chaps. The hundred men will be told to stand by to attack the guards and machine-gun posts when the signal is given from either myself or one of you should I not be there.

"Now, as to the timing of this show. I think it should either be in the morning or after late evening parade. I would say the evening is the best. The guards are slacker then. The darkness will help us to get at them. It will also be a blessing should things go wrong and we have to make a dash for it. Any questions?"

"Yes. I would think that day time would be the best time to stage this. We could then see our way up to the women's camp, and get them and the children out. I don't think we could make it at night."

"A fair point, padre. But I think we could make it in darkness. Besides we could creep up there and they would never know we had arrived before it was too late."

"Have you a definite date in mind?"

"Yes!"

There was silence in the hut.

"When?" asked Father Anjou.

"The day after tomorrow at the latest."

There was silence once more. A surprised silence. They had not thought it would be so soon.

"The day after tomorrow . . . ?"

"At the latest," said Lambert firmly.

"But," protested the intelligence officer, "the men must be briefed. It doesn't give me much——"

"The longer we wait between the briefing and the attack the more likely the Japanese are to get wind of it. Besides, if we wait too long the enthusiasm for the attack will die. It is a pretty hopeless position, you know, and the men must not have overmuch time to think about things."

"If that is how you feel, Colonel. I don't think the attack should go on," said Father Anjou quietly.

"No, I'm not changing my plans. The show is on. It has to be on. We all know the odds against us. It is going to be a bloody thing. But once we get a few guns in our hands the picture should change."

Lambert looked about him.

The intelligence officer said, "I agree with the Colonel. We must have a crack. And now is the time."

"How about you others?" asked Lambert.

They all agreed.

"Right," said Lambert, bending forward, "This is how we will do it."

They listened.

Chapter Seventeen

I

SAKAMURA sat behind Yamamitsu's desk and laughed. He was drunk on saki—Yamamitsu's saki, and Yamamitsu couldn't do a thing about it.

Sakamura had been drinking heavily. He had staggered to Yamamitsu's bedroom, where the Colonel was laid out and standing by the bed he had drunk a toast to the dead man. An irreverent toast. And then Sakamura had fumbled his way back to the desk. And he had started laughing and laughing....

And as he laughed he started dreaming.

He saw himself as a Colonel in the Officers' Club in Tokyo. He was surrounded by other officers. They were admiring him. He was the man who had quelled the rebellion of Blood Island. He would tell the story, with suitable modesty, but modesty that did not detract from his prowess. And after they had bought him more saki he would say:

"Did I ever tell you how poor old Yamamitsu of the 15th Infantry Reserve died?"

And they would say no he had not told them.

"Well, he died in his trousers with a prawn lodged in his throat."

And everybody would laugh, though they would all have heard the story many, many times before....

He came out of his dream.

He filled his glass up with more saki, and then he crossed to the gramophone with its pile of records. He began to smash the records. He hated music. It was Western, decadent. And it reminded him of Yamamitsu.

After a few more glasses of saki he wondered what else of Yamamitsu's he could wreck or take over. And soon he began to wonder where the Colonel's woman had got to. He swallowed another drink, and yet another. He tried to light a cigarette. But he was too drunk to light the match.

Instead he set out to look for Yamamitsu's woman.

First he searched the house. There were ten rooms to go through. He looked in every one. And, then, standing in the passageway that bisected the house, he called her by name.

There was no answer.

He started to smile. A cunning and evil smile.

He knew what had happened.

The sentries had taken her now that Yamamitsu was dead. They would have taken her to their dormitory. They would be taking it in turns. He became violently angry.

He staggered out of the bungalow on legs which refused to support him. He was swearing softly all the time. He would line the men up . . . line them up . . . even as they had lined up for the girl . . . and he would beat them. The thought made him roar with laughter.

Then, bellowing, and waving his stick he advanced on the long wooden hut in which the guards were quartered.

2

Lights burned in the hut. The men were sprawled on their bunks.

They heard Sakamura coming long before he arrived. A corporal said that he was drunk and mad and demented. And they were afraid.

Sakamura came into the hut. He stood in the doorway. He stood like an animal. Legs apart. Arms lifted. He screamed, "Where is she . . . ?"

"W—who, who . . . Captain?" stammered the corporal.

"Yamamitsu's woman!"

The corporal explained how he had found Yamamitsu dead. How he had organised a search of the house. How nothing had been found. Save the signs that the food larder had been raided and that it seemed possible that the woman had escaped.

Sakamura only half heard him. He had sobered up for a moment and he couldn't understand what he was doing in the enlisted men's block. He turned towards the door, mumbling as he did so. Then he staggered out with the voice of the corporal following him.

He was half way towards the bungalow when he remembered that there were people in the cell block. There was the American pilot and the Chinese girl.

And there was Kate Keiller.

3

Private (first class) Nagasiki, head of the cells detail, was telling of the one yen whore he had had in Kure the night before his ship sailed, when the news came that Sakamura was approaching.

Private Nagasiki forgot the night before his ship sailed. He forgot the whore. And the one yen it had cost him. He forgot everything.

All he could think about was how to handle the approaching Sakamura. And as he thought Nagasiki knew fear. It completely filled his body.

Sakamura lurched into the office of the cell block. The word "office" was a generous overstatement. It was a damp and depressing cubby-hole. The room was lit by a feebly burning oil lamp that cast long shadows everywhere. In the middle of the floor was a packing case. Seated on the case was Nagasiki. Around him were the two other men who made up the guard detail.

Sakamura looked at them, through drink-inflamed eyes. He hated them all, especially the man on the crate.

If Nagasiki had been born with a tail he would have made a perfect rat. He had a small and narrow face, two bright eyes and a couple of protruding yellowish teeth peeping over his thin lips. His uniform fitted him badly round the shoulders. With a theatrical salute he greeted Sakamura.

Sakamura started to rave at him, shouting and waving his hands about like a maniac. By the time he had run out of breath—or swear-words—the veins stood out on his forehead like knotted purple cords.

Nagasiki was terrified. He knew there was something wrong, but he couldn't think what.

Once more Sakamura started to screech with fury. It was impossible to make head or tail of the tirade that Sakamura unleashed. He walked across to the private and clouted him hard on the nape of the neck. His head automatically jerked forwards and downwards.

"Yes . . . yes . . . yes!" raved Sakamura.

Then Nagasiki understood. He should have bowed when Sakamura came into the room. All this fuss because he had not greeted his superior officer the way he felt he should be greeted. Nagasiki wanted to laugh, to ridicule his pomp, to prick his ego.

He did none of those things.

He bowed.

It was better to do that than risk a bullet.

"Take me to the American," rasped Sakamura.

Bowing deeply, Nagasiki led the officer from the room.

4

Joe Bellamy did not know how long he had slept. But he was suddenly awakened by a sharp bite on the wrist. He cursed in fright and leapt to his feet. In the dim light he saw a bloated rat dart to a corner and vanish. He stood leaning against the wall trying to check his fear. His whole body was trembling and he was gripped in a cold sweat of terror. He also felt terribly hungry. He felt as if a band of iron was being drawn tighter and tighter round his stomach.

Fear stopped him from lying down again. So, propped against the cell wall he took stock of his surroundings. He was in a narrow, low and windowless—save for a grille at the top of the far wall—hole. And the hole was damp: water had stained the walls and had formed dark patches on the floor. The whole place had an air of decay and neglect about it.

There was no furniture. If there had been Bellamy would have tried to kill himself with it. As it was, he found that his mind kept dwelling on suicide to take him out of the situation he was in.

He was still propped against the wall when Sakamura and the guard detail approached.

Bellamy could hear their heavy tramping on the corridor. Mentally he plotted their approach. They were at the far end of the corridor now. He visualised them pausing for a moment to get used to the half light of the corridor. Then the tramping grew louder and clearer. Bellamy found that there was something unnerving about footsteps which could be heard but not seen. They ended outside the cell. Another pause. Then Bellamy heard fingers fumbling with bolts. With a loud crash the door swung open.

Sakamura stormed in.

Behind came the guards. They kicked out at Bellamy shouting as they did so for him to bow.

"Who are you?"

The shock of hearing Sakamura speak his native tongue, even though it was badly done, was too much for Bellamy. He just gaped. But a cuff from a guard brought him back to reality.

"Ah!" smiled Sakamura briefly. "You were surprised to hear me speak English. But Japanese very educated race."

Again Bellamy just nodded.

"Where are you from?" Sakamura's voice was hard and brittle; he was coming out of his drunken stupor. "Don't try and deny you are a spy. But you will pay for that. You will be shot at dawn."

"You can't——"

"Can't?"

"I'm an American pilot. I have my papers. I'm wearing Air-force flying clothes. You can't shoot me like that——"

"What! I can shoot you. Shoot anybody," screeched Sakamura. "I decide what I can do."

"But I'm no spy. I have papers——"

"Show me——"

Bellamy handed them over.

Sakamura studied them for a moment, then tore them into little pieces. "Faked!" Then he advanced on the American. "You can save your skin in only one way. You can tell me all about the American planes you fly and what Roosevelt is planning next. You know him, of course. . . . ?"

"Of course."

The nearest Bellamy had got to the President was when Roosevelt had inspected an air force parade in Ohio.

"Good . . . you will tell me?"

The war was over. Japan had lost. Any information he handed over would be of no use anyway. Bellamy began to talk. About his plane, its fuel load, its base. Sakamura listened intently, not really understanding, but not wanting to lose face. Next Bellamy talked about the Allies' positions in the area, taking great care not to let Sakamura know that the Allies were pressing towards Blood Island. But he talked too quickly for the Jap. Sakamura became bored. He was looking for excitement. But he knew that if he killed Bellamy, and the American had valuable information, then Sakamura might be held responsible. But if he gave the American time to realise the position he would be in if he did not co-operate, he might reveal far more important secrets. And the best way to make him realise the position he was in would be to put him in with the other prisoners.

But first there was one thing that had to be done . . . Sakamura snapped at the guards, "Beat him a little. Not too much. Just enough for him to realise we are the masters."

The guards beat him.

"Take him to the officers' hut. Tomorrow you can beat him again . . . after I have talked to him."

Sakamura left the cell. Behind him came Private Nagasiki. Behind them came the other two guards, dragging Bellamy.

"You wish to deal with old woman now?" asked Nagasiki respectfully.

Suddenly Sakamura felt tired. He did not want to question her. He wanted to relax. It had been a hard day. He wanted the comfort of a woman. A young woman. Not an old crone.

He turned to Nagasiki. "The Chinese woman. . ."

"Yes?" Nagasiki bowed.

"You take her. For you, for the men. Take her to your hut."

The soldier flashed a toothy smile, and thanked Sakamura.

"Give me the key to the cell in which the other woman is in," ordered Sakamura.

Nagasiki handed the key over.

"What we do with woman when we finished with her?"

Sakamura thought for a moment then said, "You use her for bayonet practice."

"Bayonet practice!" Nagasiki was delighted. He had never bayoneted anything, let alone a woman.

The soldiers hurried away. The cell block was now empty save for Kate Keiller and Sakamura. The Jap turned and walked slowly towards her cell. . . .

Chapter Eighteen

I

LAMBERT and the senior officers had finished their questioning of Bellamy. For some time the hut had been silent. Then Bellamy said, "Frankly, I can't see relief arriving inside two months. They have about two hundred miles to push through before they get here. Now that the war is over, nobody is going to exert themselves overmuch." Bellamy had some difficulty in talking because of the bruises and cuts on his face.

"Well, nothing you have said need change our plans then," said Lambert. "We can't expect help from outside. So we must help ourselves. The Japs must realise something big has happened very soon. They have not had any supplies or reliefs through for some time."

For another hour they discussed the position. And whatever way they looked at it they knew they would have to strike quickly if they were to survive.

2

Early next morning Sakamura found the rifle in a cupboard in the bungalow. He guessed that Yamamitsu had looted it from somewhere. He found ammunition to fit the rifle, and loaded it into the ornamented breech. Then, with his pyjama coat flapping over his narrow chest, he crossed to the window.

He looked into the compound. He saw, in the distance, the lines of prisoners as they dispersed from morning parade.

Then he saw the two men who worked in the latrines only half as far away. They were behind a wooden upright but he could see their heads as they talked and looked over into the compound. Sakamura knew that they were the camp pariahs, that nobody liked them. It brought a smile to his lips. He thought that if their own comrades didn't like them, then they would not be missed. He would bag one of them, in much the same way as a hunter bagged game.

Smiling broadly at the comparison he had just made, Sakamura raised the rifle to his shoulders.

3

Dawson said, "There was a lot of activity during the night."

"Yeah . . ." Sykes wasn't really interested.

"Old Lambert ought to stop this. It could lead to a lot of trouble with the Nips."

"Yeah . . ."

"Chrissake, what's the matter with you?"

"Nothing. But we're quite safe. The Japs have never given you or me any trouble, have they?"

"They haven't really thanked us either," said Dawson.

"No, but we don't do so badly. And from my point of view, old Sakamura is no worse than Limpy Lambert——"

Sykes said no more.

There was a crash of a shot from some little way away, Sykes tottered slightly, mouth open, an ugly red gash where his nose had been. Then he slid to the ground.

It took some seconds for Dawson to realise what had happened. Then he went running into the compound, screaming and crying in terror.

The other prisoners had dispersed after hearing the shot, seeking cover as they ran. But when no other shots came they had stopped and wondered what had happened.

Dawson running towards them gave the news.

4

Sakamura lowered the rifle. He saw the wooden upright—it was really a screen—shake as the man sank to the floor. Sakamura beamed and turned back to have his breakfast.

After the meal he decided he would write and let Yamamitsu's family know that he had died—choking on a prawn.

They would never recover from their loss of face.

Sakamura was still writing the letter when a corporal arrived and reported that saboteurs had broken into the ammunition hut, and stolen some hand grenades. Sakamura jumped to his feet, reaching for his gun as he did so. His face was black with anger.

"Sound the bell! Summon all the prisoners," he choked.

5

Lambert was standing with the other senior officers in the compound when Dawson came running towards them. It didn't take him long to realise what had happened or who had done the shooting. He ordered a party to bring Sykes out from behind the screen and to carry the body to his hut.

As they did so Lambert said to his senior officers, "This could be it. There's going to be trouble. Pass the word round."

So the word was passed. From Lambert it fanned out to all the officers. From them it went to the leaders of the other ranks. They passed it on to their close associates. They all knew inside minutes. The camp grape-vine had been well tuned in the three years it had been working. One by one the men gathered their weapons and waited for the signal. Hand grenades were concealed inside jackets. Clubs and spikes were put up sleeves and dangled down trousers legs.

They were ready for the showdown.

Lambert watched them prepare then walked casually to his hut. A great excitement gripped him. His body was tired, his mind slow from lack of food and sleep. But the great excitement was there. And as it came so he felt new strength surge through him. He was going into action and the thought hypnotised him. He was going to get revenge, and the idea galvanised him. He was going to get Sakamura. He had Yamamitsu's pistol and he was going to get Sakamura with it. If it was the last thing he did he would get Sakamura. He was going to empty all ten bullets that the pistol held into that yellow body.

Lambert collected his pistol, stuffed it under his shirt, then left. He moved casually towards the main hall. When he arrived there, occasionally stopping to talk to a man or a small group, he moved down the side of the building, then round to the back.

He stood there for a moment, taking a long and careful look around to see that he was not being observed. There was nobody in sight. No guard tower. No patrolling guard.

Lambert knelt down by the boards, shifted one, the panel slid back and he whispered, "It's me——Lambert."

She was waiting for him. He saw her for a moment. Then he closed the panel and they were in stygian darkness.

"I'm glad you came. It's been terrible here. What is happening? Are they looking for me?"

"No. But we are expecting trouble, big trouble, any time now. Sakamura's spoiling for it."

"Oh . . . God . . . !"

"Don't worry. You just stay here, and you won't get hurt."

"But you . . . you will all be slaughtered. There are so many guards. And they have arms."

"It won't be that bad," Lambert lied. "We have stocks of arms. . . ."

They sat in silence for a moment. Then she asked: "You really think there is a chance?"

"Of course. There are several hundred of us." He did not say that they were all in poor physical condition and only armed with puny wooden weapons. "There's only forty or fifty of them. And they won't know we are coming at them until it will be too late."

She gripped his arm and whispered, "Good luck."

"Thanks. We're going to need it."

"Don't say that!"

"Don't worry."

Then he was gone.

6

Lambert was out in the open when the bell sounded. He started to sweat.

This was it.

This was what he had keyed himself for. There was a salty taste in his mouth. He was going into action.

Even as he moved away from the panel he saw the men were also preparing themselves for action. They were lining up. But the line-up was a loose, casual affair, every man ready to fling himself to either side for cover when the firing started.

By the time Lambert had joined them Sakamura was bringing a squad of guards across the compound. They all carried their weapons at the ready.

Lambert turned to face them. It was a casual, easy gesture that belied the tension zipping through his body and the bodies of the men standing behind him.

Sakamura faced them. The guards fell in behind the Jap, spaced out at intervals of a few yards. Lambert looked at them.

Four or five well-lobbed grenades would effectively deal with them. And as the grenades were being lobbed he would pour bullets into Sakamura's body.

Lambert shifted his gaze to the gates. The machine-gunners in the towers were watching. And the gate sentries were alert. They would be the problem. Without a doubt many of the prisoners would be killed before the gates and towers were taken.

And then there was the problem of the off-duty guards. But once the prisoners were armed with real weapons that should not present too much of a problem. They would be fighting on equal terms then.

Sakamura was speaking. . . .

"Good morning . . . though it is not going to remain good for long. It is surprising to see you all looking so fresh considering that you have had such an active night." He paused to let his words sink in.

"Well, I, your new commandant, do not expect you to work without payment. So I will pay you for all the hard work you put in. Pay you with bullets!" His voice rose higher and higher. He looked down the line. Finally his eyes settled on the R.S.M. "You, select ten men and march them to one side. Each man will die for your work during the night. Now, move!"

Nobody moved.

"So, you will be stubborn. I will count ten and then the guards will open fire on all of you. One . . . two . . . three . . ."

The R.S.M. looked pleadingly at Lambert.

"Five . . .six . . . seven . . ."

And Lambert knew the time had come.

"Eight . . . nine . . ."

A cry formed in his throat. His hand snatched at the pistol under his shirt.

"Ten. . . !"

Chapter Nineteen

1

PISTOL in hand, Lambert lunged forward. Out of the corner of his eyes he could see the line of prisoners breaking up as the men clawed for hand grenades or their crudely fashioned weapons.

Sakamura and the guards made no move.

Shock, surprise, incredulous amazement rooted them to the spot. They looked at the prisoners, stared as they came towards them. And still the Japs made no move. Sakamura was the first to die. Lambert's first shot, fired on the run, smashed into his knee. Sakamura toppled over, screaming in pain as he did so. Lambert's second bullet tore open his stomach. Sakamura's life blood spattered out on to the earth. His screaming died away to a ghastly croaking....

Lambert brought the pistol to bear on other targets. He saw a guard bringing up his Tommy-gun. Even as he raised it, Lambert shot him between the eyes. He fired twice more. Two more Japs toppled over.

Their cries of pain were drowned by the sudden noise that erupted in the compound. Machine guns and Tommy-guns began their chant of death. Between came the deeper explosions of the hand grenades, falling among the guards.

Firing as fast as he could, swinging the pistol in the general direction of the guards, Lambert reached the Tommy-gunner he had shot in the face. He dropped the pistol and grabbed the heavier weapon in one movement.

The noise was now deafening. Hand grenades were still exploding. Guns were yammering. And men were screaming and groaning and dying.

They were the dead and the damned and the dying; struggling back and forth across the compound. But Lambert's place was not there. Tommy-gun in hand, he ran towards the gates, heading for the towers and the machine-guns entrenched there.

Behind him men were dying.

Beattie died with a protest on his lips. Fifty rounds from a sub-machine-gun removed his head from his shoulders. The

Jap gunner died with his finger on the trigger. Big John felled him with a powerful swing from a club that cracked the guard's head like an egg-shell.

Mad Ike snatched a Tommy-gun from the hands of a dazed Jap. Then, turning the gun on the man, he pumped several rounds into his body. After that he ran after Lambert. Behind him came some of the others, also armed. Behind them the other prisoners were moving among the dying and dead guards. They mutilated their bodies; it was their way of getting revenge for the suffering they had gone through. Then they went on a hunt for other Japanese to kill and mutilate.

But a few, confused and frightened, sought shelter. The machine-gunners in the gate towers mowed them down.

Father Anjou, the Good Book held firmly in his hand, knelt among the dead, the dying and the damned; comforting the Catholic, the Protestant and the Jew alike. For religion knew no difference in death.

Lambert had almost reached the gates. Sweat damped his face. He wondered if he would make it. He could see the machine-guns spitting their streams of death all around him. He could see the sentries at the gates, blazing away with their rifles. Time and again he felt the sharp whine of bullets speeding past and over him. But somehow they seemed to miss Lambert. And now he had almost reached the gates, and he would be within an effective range to cut down the Japs with his weapon. Somebody behind him lobbed a hand grenade. The man had aimed for one of the towers. But the grenade, falling short, exploded in the air above the towers. Wild screams came from the gunners up there . . . and even as the screams faded, Lambert came within range. As he ran his finger tightened on the trigger and his lips thinned. His first burst threw one of the riflemen against the barbed wire as if he were a paper doll. Another spun round and round like a puppet gone berserk as bullets drilled into his flesh and bone. Then Lambert had reached the base of the towers. There he was safe for the moment because he was beneath them. He started to climb the ladder to the nearest tower. Looking up, he saw the interior of the tower, shaded by its tin roof. He fired upwards, sending a burst through the floor and into the guards. He fired again. As he did so he looked back across the compound.

Everywhere there was activity and confusion.

On the ground there were some forty dead prisoners, scattered in a number of grotesque positions. The rest of the men were streaming towards the towers or the bungalow. Behind the bungalow was the guards' hut....

As they ran, some fell, some died at once, others in a short while. But on they came, to join Lambert, to kill the guards, to get those precious machine-guns.

The first man to reach the tower was Mad Ike. He was armed with a sub-machine-gun and a few grenades.

"Let me get at the bastards," he roared, clambering up the ladder like some piratical ancestor might once have climbed the rigging.

Behind him came the other men. There was Big John, rifle in hand, legs splayed, firing into the towers. The gunners saw him, and even as they saw him the snub muzzle of the machine-guns lined up on his massive body and burst after burst opened him up from nose to waist. Others fell. But behind them came more. It was like the sea; there seemed to be wave after wave, wave after wave....

Somebody in one of the waves sent a hand grenade up into one of the towers. The tower vanished in a cloud of smoke. It was then that Mad Ike reached the top of the ladder. He was grinning broadly. The feeder swung, saw him, and clawed for his rifle. The machine-gunner did a stupid thing. He tried to swivel the awkward machine-gun to bear on Mad Ike. Ike's grin broadened. He dealt with the feeder first. He shot him several times in the face. Then he turned the Tommy-gun into the gunner's back. He lifted the machine-gun from its pivot and moved towards the ladder, dragging belts of ammunition with him.

In moments the gun was on the ground, and being man-handled towards the bungalow.

Six men in a jeep, armed with two rifles, a sub-machine-gun and a few grenades, swung past them. They braked to a stop beside Lambert. They told him that they were going to liberate the women's camp. Lambert nodded his approval. He could not have stopped them anyway. They had wives and children held there. They drove off in a cloud of dust. Lambert knew that they would give the Japs a hard time of things. Especially Stead; he had only learnt a few days before that his wife had been shot dead by a guard at the camp.

Lambert and the prisoners reached the vicinity of the bungalow. Firing came from within and from outside the building.

Lambert saw that some of the prisoners had taken up defensive positions at either end of the verandah and were shooting into the guards' quarters from these positions.

Then the prisoners stormed the bungalow. And as they came through the front, the Japs scrambled through the back, only to be cut down by the men on either side of the verandah. Lambert was delighted. He could not have planned tactics better himself. All the guards were now pinned down. And in the cupboards and boxes in the bungalow, the men found fresh weapons. A red-haired man, named Meakert, wearing a shabby fawn trenchcoat, armed himself with a carving knife. A tall Australian, named Smith, appeared with the rifle which had killed Sykes and a box of ammunition. He said that there was also a shotgun in the spot where he had found the rifle. Several men rushed for that spot.

Nobody noticed Dawson. He was a man with a mission. He had taken an open razor from the bungalow's bathroom. He was going to perform some crude surgery on Sakamura. He hurried away from the bungalow as quickly as his stubby legs could carry him.

As he left, Lambert placed his men for the charge on the long, timbered building that housed the guards. The Japs, lacking leadership, were firing wildly from the windows. Lambert primed his men carefully. Some were deployed to wait behind the garden wall. Others, with fresh arms and grenades taken from the ammunition hut, waited behind the cell blocks. Twenty waited round the bungalow, while as many again lurked within its walls, ready to bring up the rear when the attack started.

Lambert waited until he was sure everybody was in position. He waited for a pause in the ragged fire from the guards. Then he gave a loud shout. With a fresh clip of ammunition in his gun, he led his men towards the hut. All around him men were racing for the timbered building, firing as they did so.

2

Captain Salaka heard the gunfire from the men's camp. At first he thought it was an execution. But when it increased in intensity, he knew there was trouble. He ordered fourteen guards to join him.

Stead and his men saw the truck coming from the women's camp. The jeep was reversed. The prisoners took up ambush position on either side of the road. Salaka and his men never had a chance. Stead fired first. He blew the driver out of his seat. A shower of hand grenades sent the truck spiralling in little pieces towards the heavens.

Then Stead and the men headed towards the women's camp....

3

Lambert ran across the garden, firing as he did so. But long before he had reached the guards' hut, it was ablaze. Hand grenades had set it alight.

The scream of the dead and the dying filled the ears of the advancing prisoners.

Lambert reached the hut door and kicked it open. As he did so he fired a steady burst into the corridor leading away from it. Nobody was there. But men soon filled the void. In a tight bunch the prisoners raced down the corridor.

Ahead of them was a door. Behind the door they could hear movement. Lambert reached the door and kicked it. The door was locked. He shot the lock off. Again he kicked. The door swung open. He had a brief glimpse of men huddling against the wall. Then behind came a shout, and over his head flew a hand grenade. The room was filled with a great roaring and much smoke.

Then it was all over.

Ended.

Finished.

The rebellion of Blood Island had proved successful. The guards had been wiped out. Those who had not died in the fighting died in the hands of the prisoners. It was better to have died in the fighting....

Lambert walked out of the hut. In the distance he heard men cheering. And there was laughter in the air.

It was the first time that Lambert had heard real laughter for three years.

And there too was Evaline. Kate Keiller was with her. They were tending to the wounded.

The damned and the dying.

Evaline saw Lambert. As she saw him she smiled. There were tears in her eyes as she moved to meet Lambert. But there was laughter on her lips.

And suddenly Lambert too was laughing.

THE END